"You're just like Pollyanna,"

Brendan said. "You think that everything can be solved with a kiss where it hurts and a few kind words. Well, it can't."

Shelby smiled up at him. "Can't hurt to try."

He looked down into her face. "Oh, yes, it can. It can hurt like hell."

She threaded her arms around his neck and stood up on her toes so that her mouth was level with his.

"What do you think you're doing?" he asked.

Gently forcing his head down, she kissed his forehead. "Putting the first part of your theory to the test. You hurt." She tapped his head. "Up here." Her fingers trailed down to his chest. "And here." Slowly, she traced the pattern of a heart.

He knew he should draw away. "There's no medicine for that."

"Yes, there is." She searched his eyes. "It's called opening up your heart."

He shook his head. "I don't know if I can."

"Try," she whispered. "Try." It was an unabashed plea.

He buried his hand in her hair and pulled her close to him....

Dear Reader,

Welcome to Silhouette **Special Edition** . . . welcome to romance. Each month, Silhouette **Special Edition** publishes six novels with you in mind—stories of love and life, tales that you can identify with—romance with that little "something special" added in.

November brings plenty to be joyful and thankful for—at least for Andy and Meg in *Baby, It's You* by Celeste Hamilton. For with the birth of their child, they discover the rebirth of their love . . . for all time. Don't miss this compelling tale!

Rounding out November are more dynamite stories by some of your favorite authors: Bevlyn Marshall (fun follows when an abominable snowman is on the loose!), Andrea Edwards, Kayla Daniels, Marie Ferrarella and Lorraine Carroll (with her second book!). A good time will be had by all this holiday month!

In each Silhouette **Special Edition** novel, we're dedicated to bringing you the romances that you dream about—the type of stories that delight as well as bring a tear to the eye. And that's what Silhouette **Special Edition** is all about—special books by special authors for special readers!

I hope you enjoy this book and all of the stories to come.

Sincerely,

Tara Gavin
Senior Editor

MARIE FERRARELLA
Someone To Talk To

Silhouette Special Edition

Published by Silhouette Books New York

America's Publisher of Contemporary Romance

To Isabel Swift, with heartfelt thanks
for allowing me to continue following my dream

SILHOUETTE BOOKS
300 East 42nd St., New York, N.Y. 10017

SOMEONE TO TALK TO

ISBN: 0-373-09703-4

First Silhouette Books printing November 1991

All the characters in this book have no existence
outside the imagination of the author and have
no relation whatsoever to anyone bearing the same
name or names. They are not even distantly
inspired by any individual known or unknown
to the author, and all incidents are pure invention.

Books by Marie Ferrarella

Silhouette Special Edition

It Happened One Night #597
A Girl's Best Friend #652
Blessing In Disguise #675
Someone To Talk To #703

Silhouette Romance

The Gift #588
Five-Alarm Affair #613
Heart to Heart #632
Mother for Hire #686
Borrowed Baby #730
Her Special Angel #744
The Undoing of Justin Starbuck #766
Man Trouble #815

Books by Marie Ferrarella writing as Marie Nicole

Silhouette Desire

Tried and True #112
Buyer Beware #142
Through Laughter and Tears #161
Grand Theft: Heart #182
A Woman of Integrity #197
Country Blue #224
Last Year's Hunk #274
Foxy Lady #315
Chocolate Dreams #346
No Laughing Matter #382

Silhouette Romance

Man Undercover #373
Please Stand By #394
Mine by Write #411
Getting Physical #440

MARIE FERRARELLA

was born in Europe, raised in New York City and now lives in Southern California. She describes herself as the tired mother of two overenergetic children and the contented wife of one wonderful man. She is thrilled to be following her dream of writing full-time.

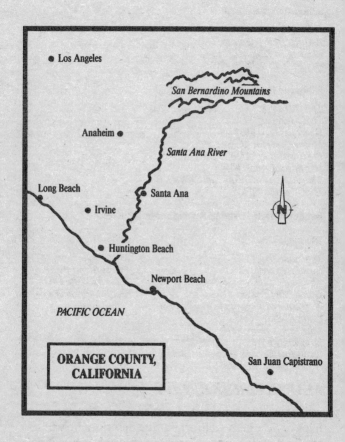

ORANGE COUNTY, CALIFORNIA

Chapter One

Agitated. Brendan Connery felt enormously agitated and restless, as if the waiting area in the hospital was too small to fit him. He wasn't even supposed to be here, he thought. The area was for people waiting to be told the results of someone's surgery. He had no one in surgery. Up until last week, he had had no one, period.

Now he didn't know what he had.

With a murmur of exasperation, Brendan wished for a cigarette. He only smoked when he was ill at ease, and then he had to light one after the other. The realization annoyed him. There was nothing to be nervous about, he told himself.

All right, if he wasn't nervous, why was his entire body taut like the string of a hunter's bow?

Angry, Brendan muttered an oath under his breath and crossed over to the window that overlooked Newport Beach Harbor.

The woman on the sofa across the way peered at Brendan and gave him a mildly curious look before returning to her magazine. Brendan scarcely gave her a second glance. Nothing occupied his mind except his reason for being in the hospital in the first place. He had been in the waiting area only eleven minutes according to the large clock mounted on the opposite wall, yet he felt as if an eternity had passed while he stood there, summoning the will to complete his odyssey.

Damn, why didn't he just go home?

He reached into his shirt pocket, unconsciously searching for a cigarette, and found the pack empty. Crushing it, he tossed the crumpled wad into a small wastepaper basket in the corner.

It would be an easy matter, he thought, to just turn around and leave the way he had come. He could walk out to the parking lot and get into his sports car, then drive as fast and as far away from Harris Memorial Hospital as the legal limit allowed.

That would put physical distance between them, but how was he going to distance himself emotionally? What did he have to do to outrace his mind, his memories? How many miles did he have to go before he could rid himself of the devils that haunted him, the bitterness that rose like bile in his mouth, the hurt that slashed his heart? How would he escape the anger that was always somewhere within reach?

There was no way except to take the elevator up to the fifth floor and finally face that old man once and for all.

"There's a coffee machine down the hall," the woman on the sofa ventured as he once more paced the length of the small room.

"Thanks." Brendan nodded absently, vaguely noting that the woman was no longer reading her magazine.

Instead, she was watching him. He didn't like being observed, although he could see why he would catch her attention. He probably looked like a man possessed right now. Either that, or she recognized him. It had been less than two weeks since his face had been splashed all over the front pages of newspapers throughout the country.

He didn't need coffee, he thought. He didn't know what he needed. He just wanted to be done with it, done with the restive, unsettled feeling that had come with that first phone call from the homeless mission in downtown Los Angeles last Wednesday afternoon.

Brendan let out a soft sigh as he ran a wide hand through his jet black hair. He had promised himself that it would be quick, yet here he was, procrastinating. What was he afraid of?

His expression hardened. Nothing. He was afraid of nothing. Fear was something he had come to terms with all those years ago. Abandonment had supplied a sturdy foundation and he had built the walls.

He jammed his hands into his pockets and absently stared out the window.

Initially when the mission worker had called about his father, Brendan had thought the whole thing was a hoax. Since he had successfully defended the venerable rock star, C. Horace Chamberlain, against charges of income tax evasion, he had become some sort of a cult hero. Phone calls were coming into the law offices in such great numbers that Jacob Montgomery, the senior partner of the firm, had had to hire two temporary secretaries to winnow out the legitimate clients.

Brendan's secretary, Rita, fielded the inquiries that were passed on to his office, and she was usually very firm with the people on the other end of the line. But Rita had felt this particular telephone call needed his personal attention. So he'd taken the call and been reeled in against his will.

It had sounded like a hoax. Just a cruel joke. God, he had wound up *hoping* it was a hoax.

But it wasn't.

Long ago he had made up his mind that his father was dead. The decision had been made eighteen years ago, right after Brendan had buried his mother and five years after his father had disappeared. But the worker from the mission had insisted on coming over, bringing with him not the homeless man he had called about, but a tarnished, silver-plated locket.

Brendan reached into his pocket, his fingers closing over the locket's time-roughened lid. He drew it out, then slowly opened it. A faded, barely recognizable picture of a beautiful young girl looked up at him. Delia Shannon at seventeen. Delia. His mother. Before the strain of being married to Danny Connery had wiped away her smile and her youth. The other photograph in the locket was of a small, smiling, gap-toothed boy. His photograph.

Brendan snapped the lid closed with his thumb and unconsciously pulled his broad shoulders back, bracing himself for what lay ahead. He owed it to his mother. He'd not gotten where he was in life by running and hiding. It was time to look Danny Connery in the face. And then be done with it.

With determined steps Brendan crossed to the bank of elevators.

Maybe it *was* time for a change, Shelby Tyree thought as she rubbed the back of her hand across her forehead. She was almost dead on her feet and there were three more hours left in her shift. Her *extra* shift.

She wrestled with the towering food cart as it began to pick up speed going down the long, slightly sloping hallway from the kitchen to the service elevators. Her arms began to ache as she held on tightly.

"Trouble, Shelby?" an orderly asked, moving out of her way.

"You said it. Can you lend me a hand, Jack?"

The short, dark-haired man shook his head as he hurried on his way. "No can do. Got an emergency on the second floor. Nothing but go-go-go around here."

"Tell me about it," she muttered to his retreating figure. *Your problem, Shelby Susan Tyree,* she addressed herself sternly, *is you don't know when to finally quit.*

The cart, which had taken so much effort to get rolling, took even more strength to stop. Shelby, acting as a human brake, yanked the cart in the opposite direction and finally got it to slow down just as she reached the elevators.

Quit. No, she didn't like the sound of it, never had. But, she had to admit, she was going to have to do something, and soon, or she was going to wear out before her twenty-sixth birthday.

The bell sounded, signaling the arrival of the elevator at basement level. Slowly the doors opened. To her relief, the car was empty. Shelby sucked in a deep breath and thought that maybe if she pulled the cart instead of pushing it, it might be more manageable. She thought wrong. Correcting her error, Shelby had just enough time to get in before the doors began to close. They shut and then the elevator stood motionless.

Now what?

She realized that she hadn't pressed her floor. Wearily Shelby leaned over and pushed the button marked 5.

It wasn't as if she didn't have an option, she told herself. Her sisters, Patsy and Irene, kept hounding her to join them. It seemed that lately all they talked about was how much more money she could be earning as a private-duty nurse instead of one who worked ungodly shifts at the hospital.

"Just think, Shel, no more running from room to room, no more head nurses lording over you. And the hours, Shel, you can pick your own hours," Irene had promised her. "That's what comes of being related to the head of the company." Irene and Patsy owned Angels of Mercy, which specialized in providing nursing care for patients at home. Patsy was in charge of hiring and reviewing the nurses they employed, and Irene, with an M.B.A. from USC, ran the business side efficiently and productively.

It was an opportunity, Irene had told her, made in heaven.

Shelby had to admit that she was getting more and more tempted by the proposition. It wasn't the money that was winning her over, she thought, feeling a wave of overwhelming weariness sweep over her. It was the almost nonstop pace that was getting to her. She didn't mind being an "angel of mercy" at the hospital, but she certainly didn't want to earn her wings at it by dropping dead of exhaustion.

It seemed to her that in the past three months the hospital never had a full staff on any given shift. And this week the absenteeism had increased even more. Today she was sure her floor had hit an all-time high. The flu had reared its ugly head. Even Josephine Hadley, the fire-breathing head nurse, had called in sick, as had Debra and Sheila, two of the night-duty nurses. Joanne hadn't come in, either, but that was something else again. Shelby knew that things weren't going well for Joanne at home. Whenever things came to a head, Joanne called in, begging to trade shifts with someone. Today there had been no one to trade with, but she hadn't come in, anyway.

Shelby frowned. She was going to have to give Joanne a call and see if she could get her to come around. Provided, of course, that she had strength enough to lift a phone after distributing all these trays.

She seriously doubted that she could make it to the end of her shift, not like this. It was her second shift in a row and her third double duty in as many days. There were only three of them on the floor today and Angela had begged off for lunch thirty minutes ago. That had left two of them, which would still have been bearable, but then Janet had received a call from her son's school that seven-year-old Bobby had taken a tumble at recess and was in need of stitches. Shelby had sent her on her way with a warning to drive carefully and had settled in to watch over the twelve patients on the floor alone.

When it rained, it poured. Ten minutes ago the call from the cafeteria had come. Someone with a thick accent informed her that if she didn't want the patients on her floor to wait another hour for their meals, someone from the fifth floor was going to have to come down for the meal cart, bring it up and then distribute the trays. There had been an accident in the kitchen and they were understaffed as well.

Feeling as if she had been caught in a nightmare that kept getting progressively worse, Shelby called down to the information desk and asked that a volunteer be sent up. Five minutes later a lovely white-haired lady with a sweet smile, a pink volunteer jacket and approximately one hundred pounds on her slight body, arrived. There was no way Shelby was going to send the woman down for the lunch trays. Instead, Shelby put in a call to the fourth floor and begged for a nurse to come up for twenty minutes. When the woman arrived, grumbling, Shelby filled her in and then left the nurse and the volunteer manning the nurses' station while she went for the meal cart.

"Florence Nightingale only had the Crimean War to worry about," she muttered to herself as the elevator came to a stop and the doors opened. She shoved the cart out, bracing herself as she pushed. "If this keeps up, I'm going to have bigger biceps than a body builder," she said under her breath.

She tried to look around the side of the cart as she pushed. As far as she could tell, there was no one in her path. Grateful for that piece of luck, she pushed the unwieldy cart around the corner and out into the hall. It took nearly all her ebbing strength to keep the meal cart straight.

The service elevators were located directly beside the regular elevators that visitors took. As Shelby struggled with the cart, she heard the elevator bell ring. Reflexes rather than common sense made her turn her head in that direction as the elevator doors parted. It almost proved to be her undoing. The unexpected movement caused the cart to totter. Shouting a warning, she fought to keep the car from upending, narrowly missing the man who had gotten off the elevator.

Pure instinct took over as Brendan tried to help the harried young nurse. He wrapped one arm around her waist and pulled her against him while steadying the tottering food cart with his other hand, bracing it with his shoulder. Despite the effort he was exerting, the main thing that telegraphed through him was the sensation of softness.

That was his physical reaction. His mental one was something else again.

"What the hell do you think you're doing?" His voice was gruff as he snapped out the question.

Normally he was civil with strangers. But this wasn't a normal time for him. His nerves already stretched as far as they would go, Brendan realized that he was a man tottering on the edge of tolerance. In his present state of mind he had little use for stupidity. And a delicate-looking woman struggling with a food cart twice her size was the height of stupidity as far as he was concerned.

"Falling at your feet, apparently," Shelby answered, straightening. It felt good to stop struggling. Her arms felt like worn-out rubber bands with little strength left in them. This man, whoever he was, had appeared just in time, though he didn't look as if he relished the part of a knight in shining armor. She did her best to offer him a grateful smile. "Nice catch."

"Thanks."

He hated hospitals, hated their antiseptic smell, their artificial cheerfulness, hated remembering the last time he had been in one. To see his mother's life ebb away. His eyes were dark and foreboding as he glanced at the woman pressed against him.

Waves of reddish gold hair framed her face, and she smelled of something vaguely reminiscent of vanilla. He looked down into her face, and the lawyer in him, the distant observer that piloted his life, took over and cataloged what he saw. Her eyes were bright blue and amazingly vibrant, given the pale coloring of her face and the obvious fatigue that outlined her features. Her face was oval, delicate, except for the slight upward tilt of her chin. Her mouth was too wide for the rest of her and it was pulled back in a smile that could be termed appealing and infectious. It gave her a mischievous, sensual quality, a combination he hadn't thought possible until just now.

Maybe she had fallen and hit her head, Shelby thought. Men this good-looking didn't just appear out of nowhere to catch falling, overworked R.N.'s. If this was a fantasy, she'd opt to go along with it for as long as it lasted.

But the warm feeling spreading through her at all the points of contact, strongly rivaling her fatigue, told Shelby that this wasn't a fantasy. This tall, dark, handsome stranger was real. And frowning at her.

"What are you doing, pushing this thing around?" He realized that he was still holding her. Taking a breath, as if that somehow made a difference, he released her. His expression didn't change. What did she think she was doing? "You're a nurse, aren't you?"

Though his voice was gruff, Shelby couldn't help smiling in response. So far, bumping into him had been the nicest thing to happen to her all week. "That's what it says on my diploma."

He gestured at the cart. "Does this come under the heading of being an angel of mercy?"

Shelby moved a tray back on the open metal shelf. Another few inches forward and it would have been served on the floor. "No, this comes under the heading of necessity when the patients are starving to death and the hospital is running with only sixty-two percent of their personnel."

He had no idea why he was still standing there talking to her. He had stopped her cart and should, by everything that made sense, be on his way. He stayed where he was. "Would you care for help?"

The nurse's smile softened around the edges and was absolutely radiant with gratitude. He had never seen anyone whose smile actually got under his skin.

Shelby let out a long sigh. "Right now I'd rather have help, any kind of help, than my sanity, which, I might add, left early this morning."

Brendan didn't doubt it. "Then step aside."

Shelby gladly complied. He was a man used to being obeyed, she decided, and she was too grateful to him to play the hearty martyr. She had stopped being hearty when she had shoved the cart into the service elevator.

Brendan positioned himself behind the towering meal cart, taking hold of either side with hands that Shelby noted were large and capable. "Where do you want these deposited?" he asked.

"By the nurses' station." She pointed to a destination down the hall off to the left. "Be careful," she warned. "It's trickier than it looks." Brendan began to push the cart in that general direction using a lot less effort than Shelby had.

"My name is Shelby Tyree." She received no response to her introduction. Ah, the strong, silent type, she thought, amused. "What do I call you, besides Sir Lancelot?"

She stopped walking and cocked her head as she looked at him. There was something very familiar about the man, but she was certain she hadn't met him. She would have remembered coming in contact with a face like that. Even in this overworked haze she continually found herself in, she'd have remembered him.

Being in the spotlight did not sit very well with him. Brendan didn't care for the renown. He just wanted to do what he did best in peace. He had become a lawyer not so much for the money but because of the archaic reason that he believed in justice. It was why he refused to take on a client he didn't believe was innocent. He had no use for theatrics or glory. He wanted to help innocent people who were wrongly accused.

Initially his client list had been small, but his success rate, his zeal to see truth and justice triumph, soon brought many petitioners to the offices of Montgomery, Shane, Dwight and Connery. Eventually his personal beliefs had filled his bank account and had gotten him a recognizable name.

"Brendan Connery." He gave her a sidelong glance to see her reaction.

Shelby's eyes opened wide. Brendan Connery. Of course! That's where she had seen him before. On television. She had seen his face on the eleven-o'clock news several weeks ago. He had brushed aside a newscaster who was trying to pin him down about his ethics. She still remembered he had stated in a low, authoritative voice that his ethics were totally intact. It was the last thing she had watched that night before she fell asleep. His dark, brooding looks had haunted her dreams.

"The famous criminal lawyer." Shelby put out her hand.

"The lawyer," he corrected stoically. He took her hand, then let it drop. "Guilty as charged." His manner cut off any further discussion.

Shelby noticed that recognition made the man look ever more foreboding. "Don't talk much, do you?"

Brendan moved the cart into position outside the glass wall by the nurses' station. "Not unless I have something to say."

She grinned as he took a step back. "Which isn't very often, I take it." She saw by the slight amusement on his face that she had guessed correctly. "Me, I always seem to have something to say."

"I surmised that." That was evident after only three minutes in her company. She was one of those effervescent people he had little understanding of. He could see it in her eyes.

"How was it?" she asked the volunteer she had left behind in her wake.

The older woman crossed to them, eager to help. "Peaceful as could be."

Shelby sighed. "That'll end soon, I promise."

"You owe me one," the other nurse said as she walked out and headed toward the elevator.

"And goodbye to you, too," Shelby murmured under her breath.

"Here, dear, let me help you," the volunteer offered.

"You're a godsend, Edith," Shelby said, reading the woman's name tag. She took out a tray and handed it to the woman. Edith glanced at the room number on the menu and was off.

"And so are you," Shelby said, turning to look at Brendan.

The laugh was dry. "First time I've ever been told that," he muttered.

But she had heard him. "I find that hard to believe, considering your profession."

"People are usually so relieved to get back to their lives, they forget to say the right words. At times I'm rather an embarrassment, reminding them of something they'd rather forget."

Shelby looked at him, appalled. "That's not right."

He shrugged. "That's life."

She stood there, a tray in her hands. For a moment she thought that the man in front of her had more of an urgent need to be healed than the patients who were waiting for their meals. "Certainly not a very cheerful person, are you?"

He answered her with a question of his own. "Always say what's on your mind?"

No there were times when words hurt and she kept them to herself. But there was no point in going into that with him. "Better than beating around the bush. But then, you're a lawyer. I would have thought that rhetoric would come easily to you."

"Not as easily as to you." He knew he was putting off going to see his father, but he followed her as she delivered the tray. "Succinct rhetoric is a tool. Constant talking is an irritant."

She looked over her shoulder, a knowing smile on her face. "To some. To others, it's a way of warding off loneliness."

Was she lonely, or was she talking about some of her patients? "You really take this angel-of-mercy thing to heart, I take it?"

"No." She stopped before room 525, balancing the tray in her hands. "I see myself as a helper, not a healer. Right now, a very tired helper." She saw the restlessness in him. "Well, I really appreciate your help, but I'm keeping you."

He glanced down the hall toward the room where his father was supposed to be. "Not any longer than I want to be kept."

She stopped, wondering. If he was visiting someone, why wasn't he going? He didn't exactly strike her as a Good Samaritan, although she firmly believed that there was good in everyone if you pressed the right buttons.

He sounded gruff, but the way he had caught her had been exceedingly gentle. And there was no need for him to offer to help. There was a tenderness there beneath that rough exterior. She wondered if he was aware of it. If he was, he was obviously doing his damnedest to hide it.

If he didn't want to see the person, why was he here? She wanted to ask so badly she almost had to bite her tongue.

"Well, I'd better go. Have someone take that down for you." He nodded toward the cart.

Shelby grinned. "I'll see what I can manage."

He nodded at her words, already thinking of the man in the room down the hall.

She watched him leave, wondering who he was going to visit.

And if he'd be back again.

Chapter Two

Brendan placed the tips of his fingers against the room's closed door, then stopped and stood there for a moment, as if his fingertips could conjure up a mental image for him of what lay hidden beyond. Emotions he couldn't begin to unravel rose up and warred for possession of him. At the final moment his courage flagged, then resurrected itself. Filling his lungs with a deep breath, Brendan pushed open the door and entered.

He looked around the small room. There was only one bed in it. A single-care unit his secretary had called it when she told him the kind of room she was placing his father in. Brendan had merely waved away the information, telling the woman to take care of the details. Have the old man get whatever care was necessary, he had said to Rita. Brendan wanted nothing more than to abandon his father just the way his father had abandoned him, but something had stopped him. Something always made the difference.

There was a serviceable table with a lunch tray sitting on top of it. The volunteer had obviously made it to this room, Brendan thought absently. A chair with orange vinyl upholstery stood beside the window that ran from ceiling to floor. It looked out on a view of the peaceful harbor. There was nothing else in the room. Nothing else, except for the bed. The bed with a wispy-haired, gaunt-faced old man lying in it.

His father.

It felt like a dream. Or a nightmare.

White stubble covered the old man's chin and most of his sunken cheeks. The lips were thin and almost lifeless. His eyes were closed, and for a moment Brendan thought he was dead, he lay so still. But with more careful scrutinizing, Brendan detected the slight rise and fall of the old man's chest.

He didn't look a thing like Brendan remembered. So much smaller, so shrunken and pathetic. Yet he knew it was him, *felt* it was him.

Sensing a presence in the room, the old man slowly opened his eyes, and even from where Brendan stood in the doorway he could see the bloodshot, deep green eyes looking at him questioningly. Eyes that had shone when he used to spin stories about what they would all do once they were rich. They were stories that had fascinated both the teller and the listener. Stories that Brendan had loved. Stories that had turned out to be lies.

The hooded eyes blinked three times, as if trying to clear the old man's vision. His expression was uncertain as he stared. The dry mouth moved soundlessly as he formed one word.

Who?

Brendan couldn't get himself to move any closer to the bed. He felt frozen, immobile. For a very long moment he stood where he was in the doorway, his hand resting on the chunky metal door handle for unconscious support. Anger, disgust, pity mingled with an odd sensation that made Brendan feel as if he was going to cry.

Except that he didn't. Not ever. Not even when his mother had died and he had watched them bury her. His soul was too far removed from the rest of him by then for that. He didn't know how to cry anymore.

His father sat up, digging his elbows into the mattress for support. His white hair rose like a wispy halo about his head. The green eyes squinted into tiny slits as Danny Connery seemed to search his memory for an image that would meld with the man standing before him. A man he both knew and didn't know.

Brendan let go of the door, leaving it yawning open as he took exactly two steps into the room. "Hello, old man. Remember me?"

Shock flattened his father's features. "Danny?" The name was whispered in disbelief, as if the old man was addressing a ghost from his past.

So he knew him. "It's Brendan now." Brendan's eyes grew cold. "I dropped the 'Daniel' from my name a long time ago." *Just as surely as you dropped us from your life, old man,* Brendan added silently.

The round head bobbed up and down slowly. Pure joy was in his eyes even as shame washed over his face. "I understand." The words were raspy, struggling out of a throat worn raw from cheap liquor.

"Do you? Do you now?" Brendan's voice was low, cold, accusing.

The tired eyes were rimmed with just a trace of fear. "Yes."

"Well, I don't." Brendan forgot to stand his distance, forgot everything but the questions, the anger that had burned in his heart for so many years. He crossed to the bed, then stopped at the footboard, as if he couldn't bring himself to come any closer to the man he had spent most of his adult life hating. "I *never* understood why."

Danny's expression was lost, confused. He looked around the room as though searching for an answer to the accusation in his son's voice. "I—"

But nothing his father could say would erase the pain, the years spent on the outside, the suffering. Brendan wouldn't let him make excuses.

"I watched my mother move through life in slow motion, waiting, hoping. *Praying* that you'd come back to her. You never came back."

"No." His voice was broken and old, far older than Danny Connery was in actual years. "I didn't." He looked hard at his son. Brendan saw the longing in his eyes, perhaps a longing for things missed, for wrongs that could never be righted again.

Brendan kept himself immune to it, to the pity that Danny's predicament generated. He cloaked himself in contempt, remembering lost evenings. Remembering pain and the guilt that was its twin.

"I cried myself to sleep every night for a year because of you. I thought you left us because of me." His voice grew still. "And then, one day, I stopped." His expression hardened, matching the steel in his voice. Danny squirmed. "I decided you weren't worth wasting tears over."

He watched his father's face. The words he had uttered hurt, as he had hoped they would. But the victory felt empty, hollow. As hollow as the man's eyes now looked as they stared up at him.

One trembling hand raised, Danny Connery reached out toward Brendan, wanting to grasp his hand, wanting to make physical contact. Brendan felt his fingers move almost involuntarily, aching to complete the circle, and he damned himself for it—himself and the old man who had suddenly appeared to remind him of the past just when he was beginning to finally make peace with it.

He stood where he was, his hands at his sides.

Danny dropped his hand, defeated. He had always accepted defeat as his due. He fell back against his pillow, exhausted.

"I'm not making excuses, boy, but I was scared." The green eyes begged for understanding. "Have you ever been so scared that it haunts your every waking moment and seeps into your dreams at night?"

No, that had been the role of loneliness in his life, until he had shut it away. It and all feeling, as well. "No." Brendan remained unmoved. "Just what were you scared of?"

"You." Danny's voice broke and he coughed, the sound echoing in the silent room. A long sigh escaped. "Your mother. The responsibility of having a family depending on me."

The man he had worshiped as a child was a weakling. Renewed disgust washed over Brendan. "So you ran." Contempt surrounded each word.

Danny's shoulders, thin and bowed, sagged even more. "So I ran."

"To what?" Brendan demanded. What had lured his father away? What had taken their place so easily with him? It was a question that had haunted him over the years.

The answer came timidly. "A bottle. Oblivion. Anything and everything that could ease the guilt, the fear, for a little while."

He didn't understand. Brendan wanted to, despite the fact that he had said he didn't care, but he didn't understand. "You had a good job. A family that loved you. It was a *good* life."

Hysteria built in Danny's voice as he tried vainly to explain, to gain absolution. "I was suffocating."

"You." Brendan's voice rose, a shard of his suppressed rage surfacing. He clenched his fists at his sides to keep from striking out. "Did you ever stop to think of what you did to us? To her?"

Tears trickled into the white stubble and slid in a zigzag pattern down the grizzled cheek. "Many a time, oh, many a time. I'm sorry, boy." A sob choked him.

The reply only made Brendan angrier. "It doesn't change anything."

"No, it doesn't." Danny gulped in a breath and it sounded as if it was rattling within the thin chest. "How is your mother?"

Brendan looked straight into his eyes, swallowing a curse. "She's dead."

Danny's mouth fell open. Tears welled up again as despair tinged his eyes. "Dead," he echoed.

How could he have thought otherwise, Brendan wanted to shout. "Did you expect her to go on, when you were her very life? You took the very heart out of her when you left. She had nothing to live for."

Danny shook his head in denial, buckling under the guilt. "She had you."

It hadn't been enough, it had never been enough and that had doubled his own anguish. Her own son hadn't been reason enough for her to live. "And every time she looked at me, she remembered you."

Spidery hands clutched at the bedclothes, gathering them into wads on either side of the rail-thin body. "Oh, Danny-boy, I'm so sorry, more sorry than I can ever tell you."

Something within Brendan felt remorse, yet he strengthened his resolve against it. The man deserved no pity after what he had done. "Don't ever call me that. And it's too late to be sorry, too late for her."

A racking cough seized the old man then and his whole body shook. Brendan made a move toward him, then stopped, held steadfast where he was by iron will. His father had brought all this upon himself.

It had been a mistake to come. He was better off not seeing him. "I'll ring for the nurse."

Danny shook his head wildly, raising a hand to stop him. "No, it'll pass." His words were swallowed up as he coughed again. Brendan crossed to the door. "Please. Stay."

"I can't."

It was too much to endure. He shouldn't have come. Brendan let the closing door punctuate his words. Shelby was just coming out of one of the other rooms. He signaled to her. "I think the patient in there might need your attention."

He stepped aside as she entered. Brendan had no intention of going in again.

Shelby looked at him oddly as she passed. His raised voice had caught her attention even two rooms away. Though she hadn't been able to make out the words, she had heard the anger in Brendan's voice. It was unmistakable. Obviously whoever he was visiting was not high on his list of favorite people. A client, she had guessed.

She didn't think he had a list of favorite people. From the looks of Brendan Connery, he was a loner, preferring his own company to that of others. Because of his looks and his fame, she surmised, solitude was not the easiest thing for him to maintain.

As she walked into the room she was surprised that he didn't come back in with her.

The man in the bed was the frail one they had brought in the other day. The one who had tugged at her heart. No one had come to visit him during her two shifts. She always felt sorry for people like that, people who appeared to have nobody.

Half the time when she came to check on him, he was dozing. When he did open his eyes, they were sad, lifeless, not from uninterest but from the things they had seen during his lifetime.

"Are you all right, Mr. Doe?" When he had been brought in he was listed as "John Doe." All the nurses had wondered why. Who *was* he?

The man brushed aside another tear that had slid into his grizzled beard. "Yeah."

Shelby crossed to his bed and looked at the untouched tray on the table. "Why don't you have a little lunch? The food here's really very good and you need to get your strength up." She smiled encouragingly at him. "Won't you eat just a little?"

Danny moved his head slowly from side to side. "Not hungry."

"Try," she coaxed. "I'll leave it here for a while. Goodness knows when I'll be able to collect the trays, anyway." She moved the table closer to him, over the bed. "Maybe something will tempt you a little later."

"Yeah, later," Danny whispered hoarsely. His voice was full of tears. He turned his face to the window. Sighing, Shelby slipped out.

Brendan was down the hall, standing by the bank of elevators. He dragged an impatient hand through his hair and moved like a man who had just lived through an emotional war.

Shelby reacted before she thought through her actions or motives. Tyler would have told her it wasn't any of her affair, but then, her brother was a policeman and used to telling people to mind their own business. She never listened.

"Excuse me," she called out. When he didn't look her way, she raised her voice as she followed him quickly. "Mr. Connery!"

Brendan turned and glanced in her direction, the fog encompassing his brain lifting enough to enable him to realize that someone was trying to get his attention.

"Yes?" he snapped, then instantly regretted it. It wasn't her fault he had been abandoned by the only man he had ever loved. Or that the man had turned up again after so many years. "Did you need something?" he added, his voice softening.

Not nearly as much as you do, Shelby thought. If ever a man needed to be comforted, she judged, it was Brendan Connery. Except, perhaps, the man in room 536.

"Yes, um—"

Okay, so she had his attention. Now what? Shelby searched for something to say. "Um, the man you were visiting, he's resting comfortably again."

"Good." An elevator announced its arrival and Brendan glanced at it impatiently.

She didn't want him to leave, not just yet. Quickly she added, "But he does seem to still be somewhat upset."

Brendan looked down into her face, his own impassive and unreadable. "There's a lot of that going around." What did this woman want of him?

"Now that you mention it—" her expression softened into a smile as she studied him "—you don't look so good yourself. Would you like something to drink?"

Brendan looked over her head toward his father's closed door. "Yeah."

The way he said it made Shelby realize that he was referring to something a lot stronger than anything she had to offer. "Coffee, tea, water?"

Brendan came to. "Oh, yeah. Sure."

"What'll it be?"

"Coffee'll be fine," he muttered, wondering why he was dallying at all. But his afternoon was free. He had no appointments, no dates in court. He had purposely cleared it, knowing that once he saw his father he would be in no condition to be of use to anyone. Maybe he'd do some research on the Hudson case....

"Just follow me. We have some in the supply room." Shelby's voice brought him back to the hospital. He nodded and followed her to a small, rectangular room just off the nurses' station. There was a refrigerator there, as well as a coffeemaker with a fresh pot of coffee on the counter.

He strode into the room and it seemed to Shelby that he filled it with his very presence. It wasn't that he was overly tall. Shelby guessed that perhaps he was six foot, perhaps a shade under. Or that he was heavy or even large boned. His was a medium frame that was blessed with natural strength and stature. Rather, it was his very being that did it. Brendan Connery made her think of stormy nights and lightning flashing across a dark sky, suddenly illuminating it.

She felt something strong and electric zipping all through her just at the sight of him. He generated excitement by being.

Shelby poured two cups of coffee. By now she was certain that black liquid, not blood, ran in her veins. She turned and handed Brendan his cup. "Black, right?"

He nodded. "Right. How did you know?"

"Lucky guess." She watched him take the cup in both hands, as if he was using it to refocus himself. She brushed past him as she led the way out of the room to the nurses' station next door.

The nurses' station was centrally located on the floor, with glass partitions on two sides, giving the nurses a view of most of the rooms. Desks with scattered papers and clipboards lined the room. Shelby glanced at the patient board, but there were no lights on. The natives, she thought, had ceased to be restless, at least for a few minutes.

She gestured toward the nearest chair. "Would you like to sit down?"

"No." He placed the cup on the desk closest to him. Then, because he didn't have anything else to do with his hands, he shoved them into his pockets. But he stayed where he was, lost in thoughts that had nothing to do with her.

"Would you care to stand, then?"

He looked down at her, as if suddenly remembering that she was in the room with him. "What?"

He looked rather appealing when he was bewildered. Her eyes skimmed over his jet black hair and wondered what it would feel like beneath her fingertips. "I'm trying to strike up a conversation with you."

His brows drew together in a thick, dark line as he regarded her. Why did he get the impression that there was

more to this woman than first met the eye—or hand, he
thought, remembering how frail she had felt when he
had put his arm around her.

"Why?"

He would ask. Nothing easy about this man. Therein
lay the challenge and the puzzle. "Because you caught
me out there in the hall instead of letting me fall. Because you pushed the meal cart for me when you'd
probably just as soon have dumped the trays on my
head."

She had him there. He felt a smile lifting the corners
of his mouth and was just as surprised by it as she was.
Probably more. "You always this observant?"

She shrugged, placing her coffee cup down. "I know
how I affect people."

"Oh?" He crossed his arms as he leaned his shoulder
against the wall. Unconsciously his tension began to
dissipate.

Shelby took note of his relaxed stance and felt heartened. "They usually find me too talkative, too punc-
tual and maddeningly efficient."

Yes, he could see that being true. He found questions
about her forming in his mind and was surprised. He'd
been in an agitated state just a few minutes ago. The last
thing in the world he would have thought of doing was
studying someone. Yet here was a curiosity that he
couldn't seem to deny.

Since he wasn't saying anything, Shelby tried another
tack. "Wanna stick around and help me collect trays? I
could use the help and I think you could use the company. God only knows when the other nurses are coming back. Janet had to run to her injured son's side and
Angela is still having lunch."

She looked up at him innocently, her eyes wide. *Beautiful,* he thought, taking the picture in almost clinically, for future reference. It was the way he had trained himself to be. Taking in experiences remotely, so that he remained unaffected.

And as he observed, Shelby talked. The woman had him swimming in rhetoric. "You really are a little crazy aren't you?"

Shelby grinned, raising her chin. It wasn't the first time she had heard that assessment. "In an endearing sort of way, yes."

Brendan laughed, his deep baritone warming her the way his words couldn't. It was a very nice laugh, she thought. You could tell a lot about a man by his laugh, even if he didn't want you to know. Beneath the cold exterior he tried very hard to maintain, Shelby decided, Brendan Connery was a nice man. Very nice.

She decided to try for the truth. "Your visit didn't go well?"

Her words, out of the blue, made his laughter fade. With one stroke, he transformed right before her eyes back to the man who had initially scowled at her.

"I heard your voices," she explained quickly, hoping he wouldn't leave. He needed to talk about this. She could see it in his eyes. They looked so troubled. "That is, I heard yours. I figure the other man was too afraid to answer." She saw his brow raise at her choice of words, or maybe it was her impertinence. She was used to that, too. "You did sound rather frightening."

"Did I?" he asked coldly. Obviously he hadn't frightened her. What was he doing here, anyway? He should be on his way. Yet talking to her, or listening to her, did provide a diversion. And he desperately needed one right now.

She nodded. "Had me shaking and I hadn't even done anything."

He doubted it. He doubted anything could make this woman tremble in fear. His eyes drifted over the form that had been pressed against his a short while ago. Not a bad figure. He wondered what she looked like dressed up. And what she looked like undressed.

His eyes raised to hers and he saw the amusement flickering there. It was, he felt, as if she could read his thoughts. There was no condemnation, no pretense at disapproval, and no invitation, either. Just acceptance of inevitable, traditional roles.

A very unusual, interesting woman, he thought, his anger at her question fading.

Brendan straightened up. "I'm not supposed to smoke in here, am I?"

"No, just outside the hospital, I'm afraid." She glanced around. She couldn't leave the volunteer alone, but if Angela ever came back from lunch she could accompany Brendan downstairs. Where *was* that woman?

He felt his breast pocket for the cigarette pack, then remembered that he had thrown the empty pack away. "I'm out."

"Just as well." Shelby smiled up into his eyes. "Those things'll kill you."

And where had he heard that before? He shrugged casually. Death held no threat for him. "Something has to."

Wasn't there anyone to love him, anyone to make the difference, she wondered. "True, but not too soon."

"That is a matter of opinion."

"That is a fact." She frowned slightly. Had "John Doe" in the other room hurt him this way? Or was it a woman? Somehow she couldn't quite visualize the latter. "You're a pessimist, I take it."

"And you consider yourself an optimist, Ms.—?"

"Tyree," she reminded him. "Shelby." He made the word *optimist* sound like a label given to fools and imbeciles. She didn't see it that way. "Yes. Among other things."

He saw that she was looking at him. "What other things?"

"Being a good judge of character."

"And you're judging me?" He assumed she was. Her quick eyes seemed to take in everything, like a computer absorbing data.

"Not judging." She grinned, tempering the word. "Studying."

Brendan crossed his arms again, waiting. "And what do your studies tell you?"

That was easy.

"That you need a friend right now." *And I'd like to be it,* she added silently.

He laughed harshly. Nothing shy about this one. A friend. Interesting euphemism. Was she proposing some sort of a liaison after all? Of course she was. He should have known. It wouldn't be the first time he had run into a pushy woman. "A friend is the last thing I need."

The look in her eyes mocked him, though she kept her tone light and teasing. "Sez you."

He couldn't help but laugh at her colloquialism. "Yes, sez me."

He patted his empty pocket again in frustration. God, he really did want a cigarette. The look that this loquacious woman was giving him made him feel as if she saw things within him that he didn't. Things he didn't want anyone seeing.

Things he didn't want to know about himself.

Yet he found himself staying.

Chapter Three

"Shelby, I'm so sorry."

Brendan turned to see a genial-looking nurse in her mid-forties walking toward them. She gave the appearance of hurrying, even though her pace was far from quick. An apologetic smile crinkled the corners of her mouth. "I didn't realize how much time had gone by."

The woman's attention shifted as she joined Shelby outside the nurses' station. With a practiced eye she looked Brendan up and down. "Well, well." A smile slid across her face as she nudged Shelby. "I guess you weren't suffering very much."

Brendan didn't know whether to be amused or uneasy. A little of each seemed to be in order.

Angela, Shelby had come to learn, was a very capable nurse, but one who was easily distracted from carrying out her duties.

"As a matter of fact, I was." Shelby gestured toward the empty meal cart, which, devoid of its trays, stood like a hollowed-out sentry off to the side. "Food services couldn't bring up the lunch cart until at least one, so I had to go down and bring it up myself."

There was just the slightest shift in the tone she used, but Brendan was good at picking up nuances. In his line of work it was essential. Shelby's voice had lost some of its breeziness. She sounded efficient, poles apart from the way she had sounded with him. He remembered that she had told him efficiency was one of her traits. She hadn't been exaggerating.

Chagrined, Angela looked up and down the hall. "Where's Janet?"

Shelby glanced at her wristwatch. "Probably downstairs in the emergency room by now."

The heavyset woman's eyes grew large as she clamped one hand on Shelby's wrist. "What happened?"

Smoothly Shelby pulled her hand free and cleared away the two cups that she and Brendan had used. Moving toward the supply room, she deposited them in the wastebasket. "Bobby took a flying leap off something in the playground and they called her from the school."

As she turned around, Shelby saw guilt highlighting Angela's broad face. Raising her eyes to Brendan to see what he thought of all this, Shelby moved out of the crammed quarters.

Angela was right behind her. "You're alone?" she asked contritely.

Shelby's expression softened. She hadn't meant to make Angela feel bad. Immediately her impatience over the situation disappeared. "Not exactly. I sent for a volunteer." She indicated the woman sitting inside the nurses' station. "Angela, meet Edith. She's been a great help."

Brendan watched as the woman in the salmon-colored volunteer jacket straightened visibly in response to Shelby's praise. Shelby certainly knew all the right buttons to press, he observed. And she made it seem so effortless. He decided that Shelby wasn't nearly as dizzy as he had first surmised.

Hands on her shoulders, Angela ushered Shelby in the direction of the elevators. "I'll take over for a while. You and your friend—" she made the words sound synonymous with *lover* "—get yourselves some lunch."

Shelby nodded, glancing up at Brendan. "Sounds like a good idea to me." She had begun to leave when one of the lights on the patients' board lit up. "Looks like room 503 wants you," she told Angela cheerfully. It was a relief to abandon the chaos for a few minutes.

She turned toward Brendan. She could see by his expression that he was ready to leave the hospital.

"Well, I had better—" Brendan began, moving in the direction of the elevators.

Shelby fell into step next to him. "*Would* you like to get some lunch?"

He hadn't eaten since seven that morning. The prospect of seeing his father after all these years had robbed him of his appetite. It had yet to return. Besides, he didn't think that it was wise to spend any more time in this woman's company. There was no earthly reason he should. He didn't know her and he didn't like being in hospitals.

"Actually," he hedged, although he was certain she wouldn't notice, "I'm due in court."

"Oh." Shelby tried not to look as disappointed as she felt. At least they could make conversation in the time remaining. "When?"

He let his excuse disintegrate for reasons that were totally unfathomable to him. "Tomorrow."

Her eyes opened wide in surprise, and then Shelby laughed softly. The sound wound through him like warm, aged wine after a particularly gratifying meal. She threaded both her arms through the crook in his, tethering him to her. Somehow he knew she would. He made no effort to disentangle himself even though normally he didn't like being physically controlled this way.

"The service in the cafeteria isn't that slow." She began to steer him toward the elevators. Out of the corner of her eye she saw both Angela and Edith smiling at her. Angela's smile was wistful. "You'll be out by midnight, I promise." Doubt still lingered in his eyes. "My treat," she added.

He didn't know if she was being guilelessly friendly or stubbornly devious and he didn't like not knowing. Given a choice, he would have initially guessed the latter, since he constantly dealt with suspects and people who had things to hide. But somehow she just didn't seem like the devious type, although she was a long way from empty-headed. "Why?"

They reached the bank of elevators and she pressed the Down button. "Oh, lots of reasons. I like company when I eat. You look like you might need cheering up." She saw his mouth open in protest and went on quickly, "But mainly because I think you're too shrewd a man to turn down a good thing."

Meaning her? he wondered. Just what was it she was getting at?

"Would you care to be a little more specific, Shelby? What sort of good thing?" he asked as the elevators doors opened, revealing two other occupants in the car.

"A free meal." Shelby stepped inside, then turned to make sure he was behind her. He was staring at her, looking as if he was wondering if she was for real. "The cafeteria food is really very good. No one has come down with ptomaine poisoning in at least a week."

Brendan followed her into the elevator. The other two people, an orderly and a well-dressed older woman, looked at Shelby a bit curiously, but she seemed oblivious to them.

"You're joking, right?" he asked.

She pressed the button marked B, then moved toward him as the doors closed. "Is it that hard to tell?"

He caught another whiff of vanilla. It brought back a memory, faint and distant, of a warm kitchen and his mother making pancakes for him. He shook his head, as much to clear his senses as to answer her question. "Shelby, I think with you lots of things are hard to tell."

She laughed in reply, amused at his comment. "Just stop me if I lose you."

He had never met anyone who could talk more than she did. As they rode down, it was almost soothing to listen to her go on. It helped numb the turmoil going on inside him. She seemed to bounce from one subject to another, compelling him to answer, to talk, when all he had wanted to do a few minutes ago was to go home and cloak himself in his work.

Progress to the basement was slow. They collected people from every floor. Because of the hour, everyone, it seemed to Brendan, was on their way to the cafeteria. By the time they had reached the first floor there was little space left in the elevator. Brendan had already edged his way over to the left corner, claiming a place by the door. Shelby had edged over right along with him. He was very aware of the fact that her body—small, firm, with incredibly soft curves—was tucked against him. He was also aware that she didn't seem to really notice. At least, there was no awkward embarrassment on her face. Neither did she seem coy, just comfortable.

What sort of a woman was she, Brendan found himself wondering. The very existence of the question, and his desire to know, surprised him. Fifteen minutes ago he would have testified that he had been completely emotionally drained. If asked, he would have sworn that there was nothing left inside him with which to respond to any sort of stimuli.

Just goes to show you can never underestimate the power of hormones, he mused. Shelby shifted closer still when a heavyset man got on the elevator, taking up the last of the available space. People murmured as feet were stepped on and elbows hit ribs.

"Sorry," she murmured to Brendan with a laugh, her chin grazing his chest. The top of her head brushed his cheek, her hair soft and silky like a warm breeze on a summer's night. A taut, demanding wave of pure sex rippled through him.

"It's okay," he told her, his response barely audible even to his own ear.

Actually it wasn't. It was very far from okay. He knew the crammed space wasn't her fault. But that didn't change the problem. He didn't want to be reacting, to anyone or anything. Not even on a superficial level. He wanted nothing more than to return to his deadened state. With his emotions dormant, he had managed to get where he was now. With nothing to distract him, he had been able to focus on his goal, becoming a first-rate

criminal lawyer. It wasn't that he liked or disliked his life
the way it was. It just *was*. And it was simple. No emotions, no relationships beyond the basic ones that required nothing more from him than his presence. The
only thing he was committed to was his work and his integrity.

Brendan tried not to inhale any more of her perfume
than he already had. Though very light, it seemed to en-
compass him. He supposed he was overreacting. Given
the situation he had just gone through, no one could really blame him, he thought.

He glanced down at Shelby. In these close quarters he
couldn't see her face. Just as well, he supposed. She had
very distracting eyes.

All right. He'd have a little lunch, then get back to the
office. Maybe it would even do him some good not to be
alone right away. He had spent so much time being alone
in the past fifteen years. Generally he preferred his own
company to that of others, but for some reason he didn't
want to be alone right now. At least, not just yet. The
lawyer in him wanted to explore the reason. The man in
him felt it best not to.

The elevator finally opened on the basement level.
People shuffled out of the car. Shelby let them pass by,
then took a deep breath as she stepped out of the elevator herself.

"Air, how wonderful." Effortlessly she took his arm
again. "Five more minutes in there and I would have
said we were goners."

He could have moved in such a way as to force her to
let go of his arm. He didn't. Of his own free will, he remained connected to this bright, sparkling woman,
though if asked why he was letting this happen, he

couldn't have given an answer that was satisfactory, least of all to himself.

They walked down the long, brightly lit hallway to the cafeteria. The walls on either side were lined with bulletin boards that boasted photographs of hospital staff members engaged in very unmedical activities. There were snapshots of staff employees at picnics, parties and distributing toys at the local orphanage. Everything always had a reason behind it, a motive. Brendan surmised that the photographs were there to instill in the families of patients the feeling that the people caring for their relatives were warm, decent people. Undoubtedly that was supposed to make people feel more at ease, more confident.

All he could remember was that people died in hospitals. His mother had.

He was frowning again, Shelby thought. Was it because of that old man in the room?

"This isn't a library, Brendan. You *can* talk, you know," she said cheerfully as she walked into the cafeteria. The low buzz of voices engaged in dozens of different conversations enveloped them as sunshine coming through the glass enclosure flooded the dining hall.

"I thought you might take care of that detail for both of us." He took the tray she handed him and watched as she placed silverware on it.

Shelby picked up another tray for herself. "If I wanted to talk to myself, I wouldn't be springing for lunch, now would I?"

The actual food area was rather small, but well stocked. Most of the people went straight to the salad bar in the center. Self-serve beverages were on the extreme right, a display of desserts and ready-made sandwiches on the left. In the rear was a steam table that hosted the day's specials: hot pastrami and chili.

Shelby gestured around the area. "So, what's your pleasure?"

You, he almost answered and wondered where that had come from. He was normally very slow to warm to anyone. It was an inherent distrust he had gathered over the years. There were women who were not shy about wanting to associate themselves with him because of his fame. He gave those a wide berth. Shelby didn't look like the type, but then, he had been wrong before.

"A quiet room filled with law books," he replied in order to deny the somewhat persistent response that had come on of its own volition.

"Sorry, they don't serve anything nearly that dry here." She pointed to the steam table. A dark-haired man in a white uniform was busy filling orders behind the counter. "How about a hot pastrami sandwich?"

Brendan shook his head. "Too fatty."

"Oh, health conscious." She nodded her approval. "Very commendable. It balances out the cigarettes."

He didn't know if she was being sarcastic or not. Well, he didn't have time for this, at any rate. He didn't even really know what he was doing here in the first place. "Look, I really do have to be getting back—"

She bit her lip. Now or never. "Brendan, who is that man upstairs?"

He had no idea how they had jumped from pastrami to this. She pulled topics out of the air like a magician conjuring up rabbits and doves.

He didn't want to go into it, but the sympathetic look in her eyes pinned him down for a moment. "Someone I thought I knew from a long time ago. But I don't."

The old man wasn't his client. She had stopped believing that when she had first seen the agitation in Brendan's eyes. "A relative?" she guessed.

"On paper." He watched as she took a piece of coconut custard cream pie from its place on the ice and put it on his tray. "I don't eat anything with saturated fats."

She laughed, moving the small, sinfully rich piece to her tray. "Don't say that too loudly. Someone here just might tap you to give a lecture on the sins of saturated fats. They hold weekly seminars on nutrition for anyone who'll listen. They're always pushing good health around here, heaven knows why." She winked. "I'll let you have a bite if you're good."

He raised a brow. She found the gesture incredibly sexy, but said nothing.

"More coffee?" she prodded.

"Might as well."

She poured out a full cup for him and took a container of milk for herself. To her relief, he seemed to relax a little, which was what she was hoping for.

"A relative," she repeated, picking up the thread of the conversation she was really interested in. "As in a stepfather?" This time she placed a large red apple on the tray. "This do? Nature's own," she prompted. "No saturated fats of any kind."

Brendan prided himself on his mind and the ability to assimilate information as it came hurtling his way. But right now he felt like a tennis player with a broken racket, trying to lob balls back while his shoelaces were tied together.

He turned and looked at her. The look on his face was dark. Unconsciously Shelby held her breath, wondering if she had pushed too far.

"More as in an absent father." He got in line for the cash register and set his tray down on the metal rungs with a firm bang. He watched as she tossed a bag of chips onto her tray before she got behind him. "Is that all you're going to eat?"

"I have eclectic taste."

"You have junk-food taste," he corrected. He studied her as they slowly snaked their way to the cashier. "Why are you so curious about who that man is?"

Her expression was totally guileless. She didn't look capable of a lie, he decided. "Because I don't like to see people hurting, and both of you were."

If Danny was hurting, Brendan thought, it was because there was no bottle in the room. "Has it occurred to you that it is none of your concern?" His tone was civil, but dismissing.

Shelby, however, wasn't about to be dismissed. "I'm a nurse. I like to see things heal."

He pushed the tray along. "This isn't some cut you can put a bandage on."

They passed the napkin dispenser and she pulled out a handful, depositing them on both their trays. "No, but it is a wound." She saw something flicker in his eyes, warning her to back off. Shelby pressed on, anyway. "And wounds need to be aired once in a while if they're going to heal."

"Both," he said to the cashier, pointing to her tray as well as his.

"I—" Shelby began to protest.

"Shut up, Shelby," he snapped, cutting her off.

Shelby grinned. "I'll bet you've been dying to say that."

Her words undermined his annoyance until it vanished. "Yes, I have." Brendan found himself responding to her grin even though he didn't want to.

"Thank you." She inclined her head at the tray as she led the way into the dining hall.

"It didn't exactly put me into debt." He said nothing further as he followed her to a nearby table. Placing his tray down and taking a seat opposite her, he waited until she sat down. "It's too late for that."

"Too late for what?" she asked, confused.

He contemplated his coffee rather than her face. It felt safer that way. She had a way of pulling things out of him he didn't want pulled. "Healing."

"It's never too late for healing." She opened her bag of potato chips and offered it to him. "That's the miracle of the medical profession."

He took several chips mechanically. "I'm not in the market for a miracle."

She smiled to herself, wondering if he knew that he was ingesting dreaded saturated fats. "Then what are you doing here?"

Suddenly realizing what he was eating, Brendan let the remaining potato chips drop to her tray. He wiped his fingers before going on. "Being lectured to by a woman who knows absolutely nothing about the circumstances."

Shelby leaned her head on her hands, her eyes on his face. "I'm willing to listen."

He laughed shortly. "I don't think you could be silent for that long."

Her expression became serious. "Try me."

Something inside him actually wanted to. He would have thought that he was beyond that, beyond the hurt, the pain. The need. But seeing his father today had showed him that he was wrong. Still, he couldn't admit it out loud. "I'm not in the habit of baring my soul, especially to strangers."

"Strangers are only people you haven't met yet."

"Charming philosophy." Brendan sought refuge in his coffee, draining his cup.

Shelby was undaunted. "My name is Shelby Susan Tyree. My mother's Irish, my father is half Swedish, half Inuit."

That would explain the slightly slanted eyes, he thought. Until this moment he hadn't realized that he had noticed that her eyes *were* slightly slanted.

"I have two sisters," Shelby went on, "Irene and Patsy, and two brothers, Tyler and Murphy. I'm the youngest and, if you're to believe my mother, the most stubborn, but then, in order to survive with that brood, you have to be. I've been a nurse for four years. There."

"There?" he echoed. "What 'there'?"

Shelby folded her hands in front of her. "I'm not a stranger anymore."

"No, just strange." He moved his chair in as several people filed by on their way out of the cafeteria. He should have chosen a more remote table, he thought.

No, he should have gone to his office, he corrected himself, instead of subjecting himself to this cross-examination by a misguided Clara Barton. "None of this is any of your business, you know."

"I know." She paused as she took a sip of her milk.

Milk. Wholesome. It seemed to fit her. Wholesome, yet almost exotically sexy. Could wholesome and sexy go together? It did in her.

"Are you going to tell me, anyway?" Shelby pressed.

Brendan leaned back, studying her. He still didn't understand why she was so interested. A slight smile outlined his lips. "I paid for lunch. I don't have to tell you anything."

She sighed. "Fair enough, I guess." But that wasn't what her eyes were saying.

Her silence pressed him to speak. "Do you always take such an interest in patients and their families?"

She grinned and he felt himself being reeled in further. "I do what I have to do."

"I had no idea that meddling was something they required of nurses."

Shelby's smile tightened around the edges. "That was pretty sharp." She turned her attention to the pie, feeling that they both needed a moment's respite.

He wanted to say he was sorry. He didn't know why he couldn't. But the word had never been easy for him. "I didn't think anything short of a two-by-four would work in this case."

Shelby raised her eyes to his. Amusement shone there again. "I'd like to see you in court sometime. You must really be something."

"So are you." He moved his cup farther on the tray. "You change topics neatly."

She shrugged as she finished the pie. "Those who retreat live to fight another day."

"Speaking of another day—" he glanced at his watch "—I do have to prepare for tomorrow." He started to rise, then hesitated. "Thanks for the company."

Laughter entered her eyes. "You don't mean that."

"Oddly enough, I do." And he realized that, in an offbeat way, he did. "It's been . . . interesting."

"You're being diplomatic." She grinned. "But then, you're a lawyer. Will you be back tomorrow?"

Her question surprised him. He hadn't thought of tomorrow. He had only thought of seeing his father once, of getting it over with and that was that. But, of course, it couldn't be that simple.

"I don't know," he said honestly.

Shelby cocked her head, trying to see beyond his answer. "Long day in court?"

She was incredible. "Don't you ever get tired of asking questions?"

"The answer is no."

He tried to follow that. "To my question or yours?" He rose, his tray in his hands.

"To mine." She wiped her lips, then let the napkin drop onto the plate. "I think you know the answer to yours. Questions and answers are the way we get to learn about the people around us. If I ever get tired of asking, I'll get tired of learning and I don't think that'll ever happen." Pushing back her chair, she joined him.

"You're a very unusual woman, Shelby."

Shelby led the way to the conveyor belt that took their trays back to the kitchen. "I think I can return the compliment."

"Mine wasn't a compliment."

She put her tray down on the conveyor, as did he. "You take it your way, I'll take it mine. Hey." She snatched up his apple, then turned and presented it to him. "You didn't eat your apple."

"You keep it. My gift."

Shelby wrapped her fingers around it. "Want me to say anything to your father when I see him later?"

"No."

His answer was firm, unwavering. The hurt behind it was evident. Whatever rift existed between them was deep, just as she had surmised. She wondered what it would take to heal it. It never occurred to her not to try to find out. Healing was what she was interested in and what she did best.

"Goodbye, Shelby," Brendan said, turning away from her.

"Goodbye," she called after him, knowing when to pull back. At least for the moment. "And thanks for lunch."

"Don't mention it," he replied without turning around. He knew if he did, it would be an invitation to her. And he had stayed at the party too long as it was.

Chapter Four

When Shelby returned to work she found that Janet was back on duty. Shelby flashed a smile at her as she approached the nurses' station. Angela was at her desk going over some paperwork, and a young surgeon sat at another desk making notes on his patient's chart.

"Hello, Dr. Hatcher," Shelby said as she entered. "How are you today?"

The surgeon looked up, mumbled a vague "Okay," and went back to his notes. Shelby knew the man was a brilliant surgeon, but his social skills and bedside manner needed a great deal of work.

Shelby turned her attention to Janet.

"So how's Bobby?" Shelby leaned her hip against Angela's desk.

"He's doing just fine." The words were full of relief. "It was a lot more screaming than anything else. Turns out he didn't need stitches. Just a good firm butterfly bandage and he'll be good as new. The teacher panicked, that's all. Nothing that a hug, a kiss and the promise of a new action-figure toy couldn't help make better.''

Janet took a candy bar out of the drawer of her desk and peeled off the wrapper. She took a healthy bite, then glanced at the stack of patient charts that were waiting for updates. ''Sorry I had to run out on you like that.''

A red light lit up on the patient board. ''That's okay. I managed.'' Shelby was about to cross to the board, but Angela reached it first. Shelby leaned back against the desk again.

''So I hear.'' Janet nodded in Angela's direction. ''Angie gave me a report, vital sign by stunning vital sign.'' The petite brunette leaned closer to whisper, obviously not wanting the doctor to overhear them. ''Who *was* that tall, masked man?''

Shelby moved to the side as Angela hurried off to see what the appendectomy patient in room 513 needed. Janet's comment confused her. ''What?''

''The guy you went to lunch with.'' Janet's eyes were hopeful as she appeared to anticipate details she could savor.

Shelby thought of Brendan. ''Oh, a relative of one of the patients.'' The surgeon, finished with his report, handed Shelby the chart for the patient in room 520. ''Thank you, Dr. Hatcher.''

''He'll be ready to go home tomorrow,'' Dr. Hatcher said as he walked out.

''And everyone will be happy to hear that,'' Shelby murmured under her breath. The surly, middle-aged executive in room 520 was there because of an ulcer. If he didn't leave soon, Shelby was certain everyone else was going to have one, as well.

"Oh." Janet's face fell, then brightened as she mulled something over. "Any possibilities?"

Shelby didn't understand why Janet looked disappointed. She felt like applauding over the patient's departure, herself. "What are you talking about?" Shelby asked, slipping the chart back into place on the board.

"The relative you had lunch with," Janet persisted, exasperated.

Shelby shook her head. "Oh." This was a familiar topic. "You're not going to be happy until everyone in this world is married with three kids, are you?"

Janet shrugged and grinned. She ran a fingertip over the three small framed photographs on her desk. "Works for me."

"Yeah, well, I hope someday it'll work for me, too." Shelby thought of her own childhood. Yelling, constant bickering and an endless supply of love. She wouldn't mind going through it again from the other end this time, as a parent. "Meanwhile, I'll go on tending the sick and the distressed."

"You don't stop doing that once you're married, believe you me," Angela chimed in, walking in on the tail end of the conversation.

"Did anyone from food service ever call?" Shelby asked, changing the subject. She knew that both women were capable of going on about the trials and tribulations of marriage for hours. She was too tired to listen to that right now.

Angela shook her head. "No. I suppose we'd better give them a call." She sighed wearily as she reached for the telephone.

"While you're trying to get someone to come up here and get the cart, Janet and I'll collect the trays. Otherwise they might stay here forever." She glanced at her watch. It was a quarter after one. "The patients should be finished eating by now. Can't have them feeling as if they've been abandoned. You take that side." Shelby nodded toward the hall on the other side of the nurses' station. "I'll do this end."

She had purposely picked the side with Brendan's father's room. Shelby left his room for last, clearing away all the other patients' trays first. She wanted some time alone with the man. Since he had been brought on the floor, she had had very little contact with him, other than taking his vital signs. He was on no medication as of yet and never rang for the nurse. All in all, a model patient, Shelby thought, except that he was so withdrawn, and that worried her.

Shelby knocked once on Danny's closed door, then again but there was no answer. Maybe he was asleep, she thought. Slowly she pushed open the door. The figure in the bed didn't stir.

"Mr. Connery?" she said softly. It sounded a lot more real than addressing him as John Doe, she thought.

He turned his head at the sound of his name, his expression vague and befuddled as if his mind had been miles away. Or years away.

Shelby crossed the small room to his bed. The tray stood where she had left it for him. "Are you finished with your meal?"

He raised a blue-veined hand and waved for her to take the tray, his gesture feeble. "You can take it." His voice was hardly above a raspy whisper, as if he had been sleeping. Or crying.

Shelby lifted the cover from the main course. There was a steak and a small boiled potato with a bright sprig of parsley nestled in between. Neither had been touched, nor had any of the other items on the tray.

"You didn't eat anything, Mr. Connery." The tone she used was one reserved for a favorite small child who unwittingly misbehaved.

Danny stared at her, trying to focus in on this woman. Did he know her? There had been so very many faces that had drifted in and out of his life in the past twenty-three years. Faces without names. Voices that echoed loudly in his head late at night, voices that belonged to shadows without faces. No, he didn't think he knew her. Why would she care if he ate or not?

"No reason to."

Shelby pressed her lips together. She hadn't surmised this was going to be easy.

"Oh, there's a very basic reason, Mr. Connery," she assured him as she pushed one of the buttons on the side railing of his bed. Slowly the section of mattress closest to the headboard began to rise. "You have to go on living."

She had never seen such hopelessness in a person's eyes before. It left her so cold it almost made her shiver.

"Why?" he asked.

"'Why' is a question to be debated by philosophers and poets, Mr. Connery. It has been for centuries. They've come up with some pretty interesting reasons." Satisfied at the height of the mattress, she released the button. "My own personal answer is that you're not going to die while you're in my care." She leaned her face close to his for a moment, as if sharing a secret with him. "It would look bad on my record."

He stared at her, still confused, then shifted in the bed, as if realizing for the first time that he was sitting up. "What did you do?"

"I've raised the bed," she said cheerfully, dropping the food cover onto the small counter by the door.

His eyes narrowed into slits as tufts of wispy brows drew together. "Why?"

"Because—" she crossed back to the bed "—I'm going to feed you. Now scoot over." Shelby waved him back with one hand. Obediently the man moved a little, though it seemed to take a lot of strength on his part to do so.

Angling the table to one side, Shelby sat on the edge of his bed. She saw the surprise on his face and went on talking as if what she was doing was the most common thing in the world.

"I know we're not supposed to sit on the patient's bed, so don't tell on me." She winked. "Sitting makes it easier for me. Besides, I've been on my feet so long that I don't really feel them anymore." She glanced down at one crepe-shod foot and wiggled it as if to prove to herself that it was still there.

Turning back to his tray, Shelby began cutting the meat into pieces small enough for a child to chew. She wasn't about to take any chances. Spearing a piece, she brought the fork to his mouth. "Okay, your part is to open wide."

"I'm not a—" Danny got no further with his protest as Shelby managed to slip the small morsel of meat between his lips.

"Not a child?" she second-guessed him. "Fine, then don't act like one," Shelby told him with a smile, "and make my job easier, okay?"

Obediently Danny chewed, his red-rimmed eyes never leaving her face.

As soon as he stopped chewing, Shelby held up another piece for him. As she raised it to his lips, Danny took hold of her wrist, stopping her. She was startled to discover that there was still strength in his grip. He must have been a powerful man once, she thought. Like Brendan.

"Everything would be a lot easier," Danny said, his shoulders permanently sagged in defeat, "if you'd just let me die."

Shelby shook her head. "Sorry, that's not allowed here. Besides, what would Brendan say if I let you have your way?"

The old man's eyes had flickered to life for a second when she mentioned his son's name. Then the deadness set in again. He released her, letting his hand drop back onto the bed. "Probably 'thanks.'"

His despair was so complete Shelby felt like crying. She swallowed to keep the lump in her throat at bay. It took everything in her power to continue sounding cheerful.

"I don't think so." She pressed another piece of steak on him, then alternated with a small piece of the boiled potato.

He chewed solemnly, like a small, deprived child who wasn't used to eating food with any sort of good flavor. "I do."

Shelby sighed and shook her head, compassion overwhelming her. "There is no relationship that can't be mended if both parties are willing to work it out."

Danny looked at her, a sheen of tears rising in his eyes. "He isn't."

She couldn't let him go on believing that. "You're wrong." She reached over to the dispenser on the cabinet along the wall and pulled out a tissue, then handed it to him.

The old man took it gratefully, wiping away the telltale trail as the tears overflowed. "He told you?" A flash of hope entered his face.

She had a choice. She could tell the truth or she could lie. Shelby opted for the lie, hoping it would turn into the truth soon. "Yes."

A little lie here, a little lie there, and maybe, she prayed, things would eventually progress on a more positive note of their own accord. Sometimes things just had to be prodded a little to get them going.

Danny thought of the dark eyes that had looked at him so accusingly, the mouth that had refused to pull into a smile. The man who had stood in this room and wouldn't forgive. "I don't believe you."

Sometimes things had to be prodded a lot, she reconsidered.

"You two seem to have a lot in common, I see. You're both extremely stubborn." Satisfied that she had gotten at least some food into him, she rose from the bed, taking the tray with her. "The only thing that's final is death. Everything else can be worked out. The trick is wanting to."

Balancing the tray with one hand for a minute, Shelby picked up the plate cover from the counter and set it over the half-empty dish. "I'll be back to see you before my shift is up."

"Wait," Danny called after her hoarsely.

Shelby turned around, one shoulder against the door as she held the tray in both hands. "Yes?"

"What's your name?"

She smiled. One step forward. "Shelby."

He nodded slightly, as if assimilating the information. "Thank you, Shelby."

She winked just before she went out the door. "Don't mention it."

Brendan had sequestered himself in the library of his law offices until nearly midnight, trying to strip his mind of everything but the arraignment his client was to face next Monday. For a while it had worked. But only for a while. Soon other thoughts began breaking in, completely disrupting his concentration until, finally, he had given up and gone home.

This morning he hadn't been able to get out of bed. It was like the old days when an invisible force seemed to keep him immobile, pressing down on him like a giant, oppressive hand. Back then, Brendan had felt that if he woke up, he'd be forced to face something terrible, something he didn't want to face. So each morning he'd try to stay beneath the hazy blanket sleep created for as long as possible, seeking refuge.

But he wasn't eight years old anymore. He was thirty-one and knew that things had to be faced. They didn't just fade away. Something had to be done to make them go. Brendan dragged himself out of bed and tried to rouse his brain with coffee.

He was still trying to pull himself together two hours later. He sat in his den, various law books opened to significant passages scattered on top of his desk. A state-of-the-art computer was turned on, softly humming and waiting for him to finish typing in his notes of preparation of the Hudson case.

Brendan leaned back in his swivel chair and rocked slightly, linking his hands behind his neck. In the midst of paging through dry court cases, his thoughts would jump back to the wizened old man lying in the hospital bed. And to the impossibly cheerful nurse with almond-shaped eyes, eyes that smiled and intruded on his soul.

He ran his hands along his face, trying to summon energy. He felt tired, drained. Seeing his father again had done that to him. Last night's sleep hadn't done anything to alleviate his condition. He had tossed and turned all night, dozing off only to jerk awake five, perhaps ten minutes later. Memories from the past returned to haunt him. Before he had gone to see his father, Brendan had been certain that he could turn off his thoughts about the situation, just as he had learned to turn off his emotions. He was wrong.

Now what was he to do, Brendan wondered, dragging his hand through his hair impatiently. Cut himself off from Danny Connery just as the man had cut himself off from him was the simple answer. The right answer.

But was it his answer?

It should be. By everything he felt, everything he had lived through, he knew it should be.

And yet...

Brendan rose and crossed to the window. Of all the rooms in the house, he had picked this one to work in because of the view it afforded him. The window looked out on the backyard. An acre and a half of lush, green Kentucky bluegrass, framed by cypress trees on three sides. Trees that hid the black wrought-iron fence meant to hold people out of his life.

Two very different people were trying to get into his life, and in the case of at least one, iron fences didn't seem like enough of a deterrent to keep her out.

The wall in his heart, however, was.

Santos, his gardener for the past three years, was working over his roses, spraying them. Brendan watched the scene almost unconsciously. It was all so different from what he had grown up with.

Brendan closed his eyes and remembered the darkness, the smell, the depression that permeated the two-room apartment on the ground floor of the L.A. tenement building. It had seemed to him that the sun never managed to shine in through the windows.

It had, though, once. While his father had lived with them. But after he left, everything in the little apartment had become so much darker. Danny Connery had taken the sun with him when he went away.

That was what his father had left for him and for his mother, Brendan thought bitterly. Oppression. The constant embarrassment of never having enough money for the rent. The shame of having to steal food in order to survive. That had been Danny Connery's legacy to him.

Brendan leaned his clenched knuckles against the windowsill. "God damn it, old man, why did you have to turn up?"

The phone rang then, its soft, insistent drone shattering the moment. Brendan straightened, filling his lungs slowly with air. He debated letting his answering machine take the call. On the third ring he picked up the receiver.

"Hello?"

"Mr. Connery," said a voice with a soft, melodic Southern accent. "This is Rita. I'm sorry to have to bother you at home, but a Dr. Hemsley just called from the hospital. He'd like to speak to you about your father's condition." Rita paused. Brendan knew from experience that she was searching for the right words. "He didn't say very much to me when I asked, but I'm afraid that it doesn't sound good."

Brendan thought of the mission worker who had come to see him at his office. Those had been almost his exact words. "It doesn't look good." For whom, Brendan had wondered at the time.

He ran a hand through his hair again, as if that gesture would pull his thoughts together. He wasn't used to feeling so scattered. He purposely had had his secretary take care of the arrangements concerning his father's hospitalization and given the hospital his office telephone number because he didn't want his private space intruded upon.

But it already was, he reminded himself cynically. It already was.

"All right, set something up for this afternoon if you can, Rita." He looked at the empty screen on his computer. "I don't seem to be getting very much accomplished today, anyway." Leaning to reach the button, he shut off the computer.

"I never thought I'd hear myself say this to a living soul, Mr. Connery, but you work much too hard."

His laugh was dry and at his own expense. "What else is there, Rita?"

There was no hesitation in her answer. "Life, Mr. Connery. Life."

Shelby's face materialized in his mind's eye, then faded. That would have been something she would have said, he was sure of it. "Don't you turn philosophical on me, too."

"Too? Who else . . . ?"

He knew she'd be surprised. It was no secret that outside of his practice he kept to himself and no one presumed to know him well enough to lecture him. But Rita was in her mid-fifties with a deep maternal instinct that had emerged slowly over their long association. "A nurse I met at the hospital," he confided.

Brendan could almost hear the woman thinking. "Is she young?"

"I didn't notice." He lied. There were a lot of things he had noticed about Shelby Tyree.

"The doctor said he was going to be in the hospital at two, making his rounds. I've already checked your calendar, Mr. Connery, and you're free this afternoon from twelve until four."

Brendan dug into his pocket and pulled out the locket the mission worker had given him. Flipping it open, he looked down at his mother's image. His expression hardened. "Two is fine. Set it up, Rita."

"Will do."

Technically Shelby didn't have to be at the hospital. After having put in three days of double shifts, she was entitled to take a day beyond her normal two days off. But Shelby wanted to be on duty just in case Brendan returned.

As soon as she was able, she had gone over his father's records, read all the stat reports and pulled together all the information that was available to her on his condition. There was no preliminary diagnosis entered into the chart yet, although several things sprang to mind when she read the admitting history and physical by Dr. Hemsley. None of them were promising.

Still, she knew that diseases tended to overlap in their symptoms and a list of signs could just as well fit one diagnosis as another. More tests were necessary before any conclusions could be drawn. There was hope. As far as Shelby was concerned, there was *always* hope. She couldn't have gone on working at the hospital if there wasn't.

Danny Connery's doctor, a highly respected internist, was expected at two o'clock to make his rounds.

Shelby made sure that she would be available in case he wanted to go over Danny's chart.

And if the good doctor didn't want to go over the chart with her, she'd hang around anyway, Shelby decided as she placed two white capsules into a white paper cup for the patient in the room next to Danny's.

She had looked in on the old man as soon as she had arrived that morning. He had brightened somewhat when she walked into his room. It had taken only a little prodding on her part to get him to talk to her and only a little more coaxing for him to eat most of his lunch. Shelby felt heartened. It looked, she thought as she walked down the hall with the capsules, as if she was making progress.

When she saw Brendan step off the elevator and walk toward her, she was sure of it.

Chapter Five

Shelby smiled as Brendan approached her. "You came back."

There were a dozen reasons why he shouldn't have. Why he should have just spoken over the telephone with the doctor in charge of his father's case. It would have been impersonal, antiseptic, removed, just the way he wanted it. Yet something hadn't let him take the easy route. And that "something" had been compounded by a desire to see Shelby again.

"Looks that way."

She wished he'd smile. He looked so much better when he did, so much more accessible.

"Angela." She turned to the nurse on her right. "The lady in 514 needs help with her shower. It's her first one since her surgery. Could you . . . ?"

"On my way." Angela went off to collect extra towels, saluting Shelby as she passed them. Her expression seemed to say, "Anything to promote romance." The woman gave Brendan a long, approving look.

To Brendan's surprise, Shelby didn't try to hide the fact that she noticed. Instead, she looked amused by the other nurse's behavior.

"He'll be glad to see you," Shelby said. "Your father," she clarified when he looked at her questioningly.

His expression registered his skepticism. The only thing Danny Connery would be glad to see was a bottle, he thought. "I'll just bet."

Shelby never even debated whether or not she should interfere in this relationship. Looking the other way just wasn't her way. She touched his arm, securing his undivided attention. "Mr. Connery, I know you're going to say that it's none of my business..."

Brendan didn't care to have people touch him, even by accident. But it didn't bother him when she did. There was something oddly comforting in her touch. Her probing was another matter entirely. "Then why get involved?"

Shelby's grin was difficult to resist. "I've been known to be reckless."

He could see that. The word seemed to fit her. He could visualize her being reckless, with the wind teasing the ends of her hair and a deep, sensuous laugh in her throat. It made him think of something else, something far more reckless that he would have liked to undertake with her. What would she feel like in his arms, beneath his body, moving to a rhythm they alone created, her lips tasting of wild strawberries, her hair like red fire spread along his pillow?

Brendan pulled his thoughts together. "That could be dangerous."

Shelby's pulse began to race, then settled down again. There was a hint of something dark and imminent in his eyes that excited her. "I'll chance it."

He shrugged. "Go ahead."

Shelby plunged ahead. "What happened between you and your father?" She needed to know. She couldn't help if she didn't know.

"You're right," he answered, his voice tight. "It's none of your business." Brendan looked around, but saw only nurses on the floor. "Is his doctor here?"

Shelby retreated gracefully, determined to bring the subject up later. Eventually he was going to trust her enough to tell her.

"Not yet. Dr. Hemsley should be here any minute." She gestured toward his father's room. "Why don't you visit with your father while you're waiting to speak to the doctor?"

The woman was a frustrated social worker. If she wasn't so damned appealing, she'd be annoying. "No, thanks, I'll just hang around by the elevators." There was a special section on each floor set aside for family and friends who for one reason or another couldn't be admitted to a patient's room immediately. He'd stay there until the doctor arrived.

"You're welcome to wait here." Shelby nodded toward the nurses' station. Janet smiled encouragingly at him from her desk.

"I'll get in the way." It was the handiest excuse he could think of. He wanted to be by himself, he decided.

"No, you'd provide the entertainment," she said with a laugh. She had seen the way Janet had looked at Brendan, as well as the look Angela was now giving him as she returned to her desk.

Brendan moved out of the doorway to give Angela room. "I beg your pardon?"

Shelby lowered her voice and moved closer to him. He caught a whiff of vanilla again and it stirred longings within him just as it had the last time.

"You've been the subject of conversation for the last twenty-four hours, give or take a few," she confided, her eyes indicating the women inside the nurses' station. "They'd welcome a chance to see you 'up close and personal,' so to speak." She saw the dubious look cross his face. "It isn't every day a personality out of the newspaper visits us."

That settled the matter. He didn't need to be stared at. "I think I'd rather wait by the elevator."

She had hoped that of the two evils, he'd pick his father's room. Her gamble hadn't paid off. "Fine." Shelby raised her hands as if in surrender. "You'll be the first to see the doctor."

Brendan turned and began to walk down the hall. "That's the idea."

Shelby watched in silence as he retreated, and shook her head.

"Strike out, Shelby?" Janet's voice was full of sympathy.

Shelby glanced at Danny's closed door. She remembered the hopeful look that had entered the bloodshot eyes when she had told him that Brendan would return. "In more ways than one."

With unflagging determination, Shelby walked to the supply room and poured two cups of coffee. Holding one in either hand, she peered into the nurses' station. "I'm taking my break now, Janet. I'll be sitting in the alcove by the elevators if you need me."

"I had a hunch." The older nurse made no effort to hide her pleased grin.

Shelby pretended to take exception. "Smirking doesn't become you."

"Oh, yes, it does," Janet called out after her, then laughed.

Taking care to keep the cups steady as she walked, Shelby slowly made her way down the hall. With a trained eye she glanced inside every open door. Patients were either dozing or watching television. One was on the telephone and waved to Shelby as she walked by. Satisfied that everything was all right on her side of the floor, Shelby moved on to what she perceived as her next assignment.

Brendan sat on a beige love seat, his back rigid. The table in front of him was covered with reading material that had been worn down by constant aimless paging. To his right was a floor-to-ceiling window that looked out on the bay. A few sailboats bobbed up and down in the water, swaying as the warm summer wind embraced their sails.

He supposed the view was to soothe people. It had no effect on him. Nothing soothed him. He felt out of place, restless, all the things he used to feel before he had found his way. For him life had evolved into a routine he could accept. He lived and breathed work, defending people he believed innocent who had been accused of criminal activities. He could put all his energy into that. There was a purpose to his life, a meaning. There were goals that followed one another.

He trusted only himself. No entanglements meant no pain. Therefore, his relationships had always been superficial, momentary. He never went out of his way to seek out companionship. If it happened, fine, as long as it was of a short duration. If it lasted longer, he always found himself so wound up in a case that he had no time for anything else. Or anyone else. Eventually the lady in question would give up, reinforcing Brendan's feelings about the futility of relationships.

His relationships with his clients were the same. For a given amount of time, his association would be close, since he needed to learn everything there was to know about a client in order to successfully defend him or her. But at the end there would always be the parting, far better than the parting he experienced as a child, but a parting nonetheless.

His father, his entire past, breaking in on him the way it had had unnerved Brendan, unsettled his structured life. It was as if, for some reason, he had discovered that his foundations were built on sand. His father's appearance had brought the rains, threatening to wash away everything he had worked for, everything he had created.

He wanted peace, he thought, staring out the window. God, he longed for peace. He found none now. The gnarled old man lying in that hospital bed a few feet away wouldn't let him have it. His father had taken it away from him once in his youth and now the old man had returned to undo all that Brendan had worked so hard to achieve. Brendan supposed that until the question of his father's health was satisfactorily resolved and he could send the man on his way with a few dollars in his pocket, there would be no peace, not for him.

Brendan sensed Shelby's presence before he actually turned and saw her. He had no idea why he knew it was her, or even why he knew that someone had approached. The floors were carpeted with that durable,

bland floor covering that showed nothing and camou-
flaged everything. It effectively swallowed up the sound
of footsteps.

Yet he had heard her.

The expression on his face was dark and brooding
when he turned to look at her. Shelby thought that she
had seen few people hurting the way Brendan was.

"I brought you coffee." She stood before him, offering him his choice.

He accepted the cup closest to him. He took a long sip,
certain that he'd need the caffeine now that she was here.
"Have you got some kind of vested interest in the coffee bean industry?"

She glanced toward the window. There was a pigeon
strolling along the windowsill. She turned her glance to
Brendan. "No, why?" She lifted the cup to her lips and
drank.

"You're always pushing coffee on me." He raised the
cup for emphasis.

A smile grew behind the cup. Her eyes joined it.
"Makes for a good icebreaker."

As if she needed one. "No tottering food carts available today?"

"None, thank goodness." Shelby sat down beside
Brendan. Her thigh touched his as she leaned back. They
both felt the electricity pass between them. "Today's
chaos is on a more controlled level. I'm happy to report
that the patients all received their trays on schedule. Do
you mind if I sit down?"

He looked at her incredulously. She was seeking permission after the fact. "You already are."

Shelby took her cup in both hands and toyed with it.
"Just thought I'd give you an option."

Brendan looked past her to the window ledge. The pigeon had been joined by a friend and they were both marching back and forth as if it were some sort of mating ritual.

"I don't seem to have very many," Brendan answered, thinking of the turn his life had taken in the past few days.

She knew he was talking about his father. "He ate both his meals today."

"Uh-huh." Brendan continued staring off into space. He didn't want to care if his father ate or if he bathed or if he even existed. He *didn't* want to care. Couldn't she understand that? How could she, he thought in exasperation. She didn't know.

Shelby pressed on, just as she had with his father when he had refused to eat. "I had to feed him yesterday, but he's coming around a little."

Brendan finally looked at her. "Why did you have to feed him? He's not an invalid."

She kept her gaze steady as she looked into his eyes. "I guess that would be a matter of perspective, Mr. Connery." And then a small smile flitted over her lips. "Besides, he wouldn't eat. He said it'd be better for everyone if he just died."

The starkness of the remark jolted him, but he kept his reaction to himself. The old man probably knew which strings to pull with someone like Shelby. He couldn't have survived in his nomadic condition for as long as he had if he didn't. "Maybe he's right."

Shelby stared at him, stunned. No, she wasn't going to believe he meant that. He couldn't. That was the hurt talking. "I told him he couldn't do it while he was on my floor. I wouldn't stand for it."

Brendan laughed. The woman's moxie was not to be believed. "So now you're in charge of life and death as well as meal trays?"

Shelby took another drink of her coffee. It was cooling quickly. "No," she answered softly, "I'm in charge of trying to eradicate depression if I can. I think he just needed someone to pay attention to him." She looked at Brendan meaningfully. "He still does."

She wasn't going to reel him in. "He's not the only one who's ever felt that."

"Then I'd think the solution would be rather simple." She placed her hand on top of his.

The sensation the touch of her hand created warred with the anger he felt at her intrusion. Why couldn't she simply be a beautiful woman he had met somewhere instead of a nurse bent on being an angel of mercy?

"No, Shelby, the solution is anything but simple. Look, if you're trying to make me feel guilty—"

"I can't do that," she said quietly. "Only you can do that."

He put his cup down on the table. Had it been made of china, it would have cracked. "I don't have anything to feel guilty about."

It was hard not to drop her gaze. There was anger in his eyes, a sense of power, determination. She could see why he made a good attorney, but she stood her ground. "Abandoning someone in need is sufficient reason."

Anger rose in his eyes like a flame. "Why don't you talk to him about that if you want some inside information on abandonment?"

The elevator bell rang and a moment later a small, genial-looking man wearing an ill-fitting, dark blue suit stepped off.

Shelby saw the question on Brendan's face and met the respite with relief. She nodded to his unspoken inquiry. "That's Dr. Hemsley."

"That?" The man looked more like a tired, rumpled shopkeeper than a highly recommended doctor. Brendan wondered if someone had steered his secretary wrong when she had made her initial inquiries at the hospital before having his father admitted.

"Don't let the suit fool you," Shelby whispered. "Everything else about him is sharp. He's too concerned about his patients to take the time to spend on his appearance." She got off the love seat, stacking one cup inside another.

Brendan rose as the man passed by. "Dr. Hemsley?" he asked.

The man turned at the sound of his name. The gray eyes were kind, set within a face that had earned more than its share of lines in his twenty-odd years of practice. "Yes?"

Brendan came forward. "I'm Brendan Connery." He put out his hand. "Danny Connery is a patient of yours. Danny is my—" he stopped.

The word wouldn't come. It had been so long since he had uttered the name *father* in reference to Danny. It didn't seem as if it belonged.

"Father," Shelby prompted gently, giving his hand a squeeze.

Brendan wanted to pull his hand away. Yet he didn't. He couldn't. Unconsciously he felt himself drawn to the life force Shelby radiated, and he left his hand in hers.

If Dr. Hemsley thought it odd that Brendan needed someone to supply the word that described his connection to Danny Connery, he didn't show it.

"Yes, of course." He shook Brendan's hand heartily. "Come with me. I believe his chart is at the nurses' station." The doctor peered over his rimless glasses at Shelby for confirmation.

Shelby nodded and moved ahead of the two men, feeling it best to leave them together.

Angela and Janet looked surprised to see Shelby returning so soon from her break. The questions that sprang up died when they saw that Dr. Hemsley was with her, walking next to Brendan. Shelby could feel their curiosity, but both women went about their work in silence.

"I'm afraid that your father's a very worn-out old man," Dr. Hemsley told Brendan. Shelby handed Danny's chart to him, and Dr. Hemsley flipped through the pages one by one to refamiliarize himself with the case. "Standard tests haven't shown us very much except that he has the body of a man fifteen years older than he is chronologically. There's been a great deal of abuse going on for a long time."

"He drinks." Brendan offered the information without emotion.

"So I gather." The doctor turned to another page, shaking his head. "Excessively and for a long period of time." He flipped the pages back and closed the chart, then tucked it under his arm. Linking his fingers together before him, he looked compassionately at Brendan. "I don't mean to be so blunt—"

"By all means." Brendan waved away his apology. "Be blunt."

"This sort of abuse has to come to a stop. His liver and kidneys are barely functioning. His heart is suffering. And he appears to have the beginnings of a great number of problems."

"I'd say it was more than the beginning," Brendan said, more to himself than to the doctor.

The doctor looked up sharply. Shelby was standing off to the side, checking over the medication schedule. She was keeping one eye on the scene playing out near the hallway and she saw the surprise in the older man's eyes at Brendan's bitter tone.

"Yes, well." Dr. Hemsley cleared his throat and placed the chart on top of the closest desk. "I'd like to do a laparoscopy on him. With your permission, of course. I assume you're the responsible party."

Brendan took a moment before he answered. It felt odd being responsible for a man he hadn't seen for so many years. A man he had hated....

"Yes, I suppose I am." He looked down at the doctor. "Just what is a laparoscopy? Another test?"

"Surgery," the doctor corrected. "Of the most innocuous type, I assure you. In effect, it's to explore an area of the body via a powerful microscope we slip in through a tiny slit in the abdomen. It's relatively simple and it tells us a great deal."

Brendan nodded as he took a deep breath. Nothing was ever simple when it concerned Danny. He had thought that perhaps this was all just an act, perpetrated by Danny and the mission employee to possibly get money out of him. After all, there were those articles about him in the paper after the last trial. And he was well-off.

But it wasn't an act. There was something obviously wrong.

He turned to look at the doctor again. "When would you do it?"

Dr. Hemsley looked relieved at Brendan's compliance. "As soon as I can arrange for an O.R. team to assist me. Possibly as soon as seven-thirty tomorrow morning if you're agreeable.''

Brendan shrugged. The sooner the better. It made no difference to him. ''Go ahead. Do what you have to do.''

Dr. Hemsley opened his mouth to say something further, then obviously decided against it. He turned to use the telephone on Shelby's desk. But the doctor paused before he began dialing. ''I'll be in to see your father in a few minutes. Would you rather tell him about the operation yourself or shall I?''

Brendan turned, his back to Danny's door. He wanted no part of that. ''I think you're better equipped to handle that.''

The doctor nodded and pressed the buttons on the telephone that connected him to the woman who coordinated the operating room staff.

Shelby came up behind Brendan and placed her hand on his shoulder. ''It'll be all right,'' she told him. ''It's just a routine procedure.''

''Whatever.'' He shrugged carelessly.

Too carelessly, Shelby thought. It was a studied move and she didn't buy it. ''Brendan, I know you have to feel something.''

He took hold of her shoulders and moved her until they both stood in the hall, away from the others. ''What I feel is not what you think.'' The look in his eyes warned her not to go any further.

Shelby had never been any good at taking warnings. ''Then tell me what to think.''

He dropped his hands, afraid that he might be hurting her, that his anguish might transfer itself through his very touch. ''Why are you so involved?'' *Why can't you just let it be,* he added silently.

She wanted to reach out and touch his cheek, to stroke, to soothe. But she knew he wouldn't let her. Not yet.

"Because I am, that's all." She looked at him significantly, imploring him to let go of his anger. "Someone has to be. For both your sakes."

He laughed and shook his head. She was incapable of understanding. "This goes way beyond bedpans and pills, Shelby."

"Good, that's the part I like." She grinned, relieved to see the anger abating. "More coffee?"

He had to laugh then, really laugh, releasing some of the tension that had him so rigid. "You don't give up, do you?"

She shook her head and her hair bounced like a flaming cloud about her face. "Haven't the slightest idea what the phrase means."

Beneath the turmoil that was raging through him was a persistent yearning to draw comfort from this woman he hardly knew. This woman who, when she smiled, seemed to remove some of the dark gloom he carried with him.

He realized that, more than anything, he wanted to make love with her.

"Are you free tonight?" he asked.

The question, coming out of the blue, surprised her. "In what capacity?"

The look he gave her was meaningful. "I don't need a nurse."

She felt something warm blossoming inside her. "I double as a woman."

"That was the capacity I was thinking of." He touched the ends of her hair. It was enough for now. "I'd like to share something besides coffee with you."

Her eyes held his. A promise of things to come awoke within her. "You're on, Brendan."

It was one of the few times she had used his name and there was something soft and alluring about the way it sounded on her lips. His breath caught in his throat as he visualized her the way he wanted her.

"If you give me your address, I'll be by at eight to pick you up."

She had been up since three this morning. By eight she was usually winding down, preparing to go to bed. No matter. She'd been surviving on five hours' sleep a night for the past four days.

"Eight will be fine."

The doctor passed them on his way to Danny's room.

Shelby bit her lower lip. "I really think you should say a few words to your—to Danny," she amended when she saw the warning look in Brendan's eyes.

But Brendan shook his head. "It's past the time for words."

He just couldn't put her off with his arguments. "You above all people should know it's never too late for words. Or else lawyers would be out of a job."

But she wasn't going to convince him. He was involved as much as he intended to be. Too much so. "Then you do it. I can't."

Shelby knew she had to let it go for now. But in her heart she promised herself that this was a topic they'd get back to. They had to.

Chapter Six

On her way home Shelby stopped by Angels of Mercy, Irene and Patsy's home nursing care agency. It was located only a couple of miles from Harris Memorial. In its third year, the business Irene had begun on a whim was thriving, with more than its share of referrals. The nurses were competent and hardworking, and the quality of care was beyond reproach. Patsy was always on the lookout for more nurses who met her high standards.

Which was why the number of phone calls to her home had increased, Shelby thought as she spied an available parking space not too far from the front entrance of the tall building.

Pulling her car in beside a station wagon that had been involved in a recent car accident and had obviously gotten the worst of the encounter, Shelby got out and hurried to the double glass doors. She pushed them open and made a sharp left to the office. Directly opposite was

a pharmacy. All the rest of the office space was occupied by physicians associated with Harris Memorial.

The Angels of Mercy reception area was decorated
with a calculating eye. Irene had overseen it all herself.
The colors were earthy browns and oranges, peaceful,
soothing. Tall, leafy plants flourished and thrived in two
of the four corners. Shelby knew that Irene and Patsy
had hired someone to come and care for the plants on a
regular basis. Between the two women there wasn't a
single green thumb to be had. Their talents existed else-
where.

Shelby made it a habit to drop by her sisters' office
once or twice a week before going home. This week had
been particularly long so she hadn't had a chance,
prompting more phone calls from Irene. Since Shelby
had met Danny Connery—and Brendan—Irene's proposition about joining the nursing agency was taking on
more and more of a persuasive edge.

Irene was at the receptionist's desk, overseeing last-
minute details. Irene Tyree Walker was as dark as Shelby
was fair, taking after their father's side of the family. She
had glossy jet black hair, which she always wore pulled
back and secured with two ornamental clips. Her face,
although slight, was not quite as delicate as Shelby's.
Her clothing was expensive but not flashy. There were
more differences than similarities between the two
women. But when Irene smiled, all doubts of a family
resemblance faded.

Irene looked up when the tinkling sound of the door
chime announced Shelby's arrival. The smile that came
so easily to Irene's lips filled out even more when she saw
her youngest sister.

"I'll need that in triplicate, Tina," Irene said to the
young secretary hovering over her. She handed Tina the

packet of documents she was holding. "New contracts," Irene explained to Shelby.

That attended to, Irene rose and took Shelby's hands in hers. Nine years older, Irene was the shorter of the two by four inches.

"So," she asked, her sharp eyes absorbing every nuance, especially the vibrant look in Shelby's own eyes, "is it yes?"

Shelby laughed. "Irene, you certainly are pushy when you want to be."

"Sorry." Irene released her sister's hands and patted Shelby's cheek. "It runs in the family." Irene took her seat behind the light oak desk again.

Rocking back slightly, she studied Shelby for a moment. They knew each other inside and out and could tell when something was on the other's mind. Something was on Shelby's now.

"What'll it be, Shel? Slaving away for someone else, or building for the future?"

Shelby dropped into the curved, upholstered rust chair opposite her sister's desk. It felt good to get off her feet. "You'd make a good politician, Irene."

Irene accepted it as her due. It was Irene who had the business sense in the family, who could second-guess things and make sure they turned out well. "Then cast your vote this way."

If she was to be honest with herself, Shelby knew she had come this time not just to say hello, but to be persuaded to leave the hospital, to have any doubts erased and the balance tipped irrevocably. But Shelby wondered at her sister's reasons for pushing so hard for her to resign. After all, she had never complained about her lot at the hospital, although Patsy, who had worked at

Harris with her for several years, had brought tales of difficult conditions home to the dinner table.

"Why are you so eager to get me to leave the hospital? I like it there, Irene."

The answer for Irene was simple. "Frankly, I always saw all of us as being successes." She pushed herself away from her desk and rose.

"That doesn't always mean money," Shelby pointed out, glancing down at the expensive imported leather shoes Irene was wearing. For Shelby it had never been a matter of money. It had been a matter of making a difference, of helping.

Irene grinned. "No, but having money certainly doesn't hurt, either." She came up behind Shelby and put her hands on Shelby's shoulders. "You're my little sister. I don't want you throwing away your energy on something that'll never get you anywhere. Fifteen years from now you could still be on the night shift."

Shelby turned in her seat to see Irene's face. "I'm not *on* the night shift now."

"See, you'll be demoted." Moving to stand in front of Shelby, Irene continued talking. "I've just made arrangements to get us a great health plan, and the benefits from being with the company—"

Irene was not one to sit back and relax, Shelby thought. "You already sound like a high-powered executive."

"Sugar," Irene said adjusting her bracelet, "I *am* a high-powered executive. I've just got to get the company up to par to match me." She tapped her temple. "It's all a state of mind. Now." She sat on the edge of her desk, assuming a higher vantage point to conduct the discussion. "What sort of state is your mind in?"

Because there was always a pleasant, but nonetheless vital sisterly rivalry going on between them, Shelby wanted Irene to work just a little harder in winning her over. Handing a victory to Irene with no opposition always disappointed her. She liked winning after a good match, not due to default. "I promise I'll think about it."

Irene crossed her arms in front of her. "That's what you said the last time I talked to you."

"No, this time I'll *really* think about it." Because Irene looked as if she expected more, Shelby added, "Something's come up."

Irene sat up a little straighter, eyes alert. "Male something?" she probed hopefully.

Shelby maintained a poker face. "The patient is a man, yes."

Of the five of them, Shelby was the only one who still wasn't married. Irene, better than anyone, knew all the love Shelby had to offer. She maintained that Shelby needed to find someone to channel that love to, rather than pouring it out on patients who floated in and out of her life. It just wasn't fruitful that way. Irene believed in things being fruitful. "So far, it sounds promising."

Shelby let her grin surface. "He's sixty-three years old."

"Another promise bites the dust." Irene hopped off the desk and moved around behind it. She picked up a file and tucked several letters into it. "What is it about this sixty-three-year-old patient that's changed your perspective?" she asked casually.

Shelby thought of Danny, compassion igniting within her as his face materialized in her mind. "I think he's going to need care once he's discharged. I can't help him if I have a regular job. And I want to help.''

Irene dropped the folder into the file cabinet and pushed the drawer closed slowly. When she turned, she looked at Shelby thoughtfully. "There's more to this than you're telling me, isn't there?''

There were no secrets in the Tyree family. Not for long. "What makes you say that?''

Irene laughed. The answer was so transparent. "Out of all of us, you were always the one with the softest heart, the one who cried over holiday greeting-card commercials where the families welcomed each other with open arms around a Christmas tree.'' There was no smug criticism, no cynicism in the observation Irene made. The affection in her voice was unmistakable.

Shelby shrugged. "The man needs someone to care about him, and his son—''

Intrigued again, Irene's grin was wide. "Oh, there's a son.''

Shelby knew exactly what her sister was thinking. It seemed to her that the whole world had turned into Johnny One-Note when it came to the subject of her marital status. "Yes, there's a son.''

"Unattached?'' Irene prodded.

Shelby sighed. "That's not the important part.'' Not at the moment, anyway. Shelby was thinking of Danny's needs, not Brendan's. Or hers.

Irene shrugged, trying to seem sophisticatedly uninterested. Shelby knew her better than to be taken in. "It is to his wife if he has one.''

Shelby decided to be kind and give Irene more details. "He doesn't.''

"Better and better.''

She had come here to make a decision, if possible, about her career and about an old man who needed help. Irene was planning orange blossoms. "Irene, are you going to get serious?"

The broad smile faded just a little, not in anger, but to be replaced by sincerity. "Shel, where someone from my family is involved, I'm *always* serious." Irene looked at her younger sister closely. "Is it?"

Shelby glanced at her watch. She hadn't budgeted her time well, but then, she hadn't expected to get into a debate about her love life. "Is it what?"

"Serious?"

She wasn't sure she was following Irene anymore. "With who?"

"With the sixty-three-year-old man." Irene threw up her elegantly manicured hands. "With his *son,* dummy."

Yes, I think so. Maybe. Oh, who knows, Shelby thought, her mind ricocheting from one point to another. "Irene." She looked at her sister impatiently. "I've only seen the man twice."

"Sometimes things work their way up to a slow simmer, sometimes they boil right over at the start." Irene looked into her face, looking for her answer. "Which is it?"

Shelby rose. It was getting late. "We're working our way up to a simmer. Satisfied?" No more beating around the bush. She didn't have time for it. "Now, do you want to know my plans, or not?"

The phone rang. Irene held up a warning finger for Shelby not to take the opportunity to leave. "I'm waiting with bated breath. Angels of Mercy," she said into the receiver. "Can you hold a moment, please? Thank you." Irene pressed a button down. "Talk," she ordered Shelby.

"I'll hand in my resignation at Harris right after Mr. Connery's discharged." She realized that she had actually made up her mind about the matter before she had even stopped by Irene's.

Irene threw her arms around Shelby. "Welcome aboard, Shel. You won't regret this—and neither will the patients who need you. And after a little while Patsy and I will bring you into the executive end of the business."

But Shelby had no desire to become a reigning businesswoman. Being a nurse suited all her wants and needs. She knew that raising this point would embroil her in another debate with Irene, and she had no time for that.

Irene's finger hovered over the flashing Hold button. "Why don't you let me take this call and then we can phone Patsy with the good news. She's taken the day off—another privilege of management." Irene winked.

Shelby shook her head. "Can't." She gathered her purse to her as she edged her way to the door. "I've got to go home and get ready."

Irene bit her lower lip and looked at Shelby hopefully. "Got a date?"

"Yes."

"Shelby, I've never known you not to be talkative. Is it the sixty-three-year-old's son?"

They couldn't keep referring to him that way. Besides, if she could talk Brendan into it, he was going to be hiring her through the company shortly. "His name is Brendan."

Irene grinned broadly. "I always liked that name."

"Yeah, sure." Shelby opened the front door. Irene would like the name Mordred if it meant Shelby was dating him.

"Have a good time, Shel," Irene called after her.

"Answer your flashing light, Irene," Shelby replied as she left.

He had too much on his mind these days. Brendan wondered if he was doing a disservice to his clients. Perhaps he could split his caseload among the other lawyers at the firm until the turmoil within his life was satisfactorily resolved.

No. He dismissed the thought in exasperated anger. Handing over his clients to someone else would be shirking his responsibility. That wasn't him. He had hated his father for that. To do so would be putting himself in the same category as Danny Connery.

Brendan sighed as he made a right turn on MacArthur Boulevard. He didn't really have time for this date tonight.

Date.

What an outmoded word, he mused with a deprecating smile on his lips. But there wasn't a better one to put in its place. It was a date. He had actually asked a woman out for no other reason than that she was there and he had wanted to share an evening with her. Usually, if he socialized at all, it was at a function to which he felt obligated to bring a partner. Because of his wide range of acquaintances, there was always someone to ask. One was as good as another.

He couldn't remember the last time he had wanted to be with a woman just to *be* with her. He'd had his share of liaisons, of physical relationships that had lasted for a time, but they'd all been superficial, which was just the way he had wanted them. No woman had lingered on his mind, interrupting his thoughts or making him smile unexpectedly when he thought of her.

Until now.

Shelby was impossibly argumentative and stubborn and hopelessly curious. And he was anticipating seeing her, just like a teenager.

At least, he supposed this was the way teenagers reacted. He had never had time to be one. His mother's death had left him to be passed from one home to another, to raise himself as best he could until he was of age, in the court's eyes, to take responsibility for himself. In his own eyes he had done that the day his father had left.

Annoyed with his reactions, Brendan's hand hovered over the car phone. He could just call Shelby and tell her that something had come up. Things were always coming up, he thought cynically. Just look at last week.

He replaced his right hand on the steering wheel again. He didn't want to tell Shelby that something had come up. He wanted to see this evening through, no matter where it led. He wanted to see *her,* to explore these strange new sensations she aroused in him. He had never run from anything before.

Except his own feelings.

Brendan pulled in front of a large, Mediterranean-style condominium. The number on the front matched the address she had given him. With a hand that wasn't completely steady he shut off the engine, then sat in the stilled car, going over a final debate in his mind. He had a heavy caseload and an apparition from his past to tax him. He didn't need anything extra in his life.

But he couldn't quite make himself turn his back on Shelby and just drive away. He couldn't explain why. Maybe it was curiosity. Maybe it was a survivor's instinct that told him that he did need something extra in his life. He had absolutely no idea. He only knew that he couldn't turn away.

Brendan got out of his car and slammed the door behind him decisively. The driveway was paved with cobblestones. Very picturesque, he thought. It fit her.

An impressive flight of stairs led to the front door. It was obvious that the people who visited Shelby were in hearty condition.

The stress he had experienced today became evident to Brendan as he climbed the steep stairs. He rang the bell and barely heard the melodic chimes before the door flew open.

"Were you standing behind the door?" She couldn't possibly have been standing anywhere else in the house and reached the door so quickly.

"Yes I was," Shelby said, taking his arm and ushering him inside.

He was surprised at her unabashed honesty. People weren't generally this open, at least not in his experience.

"I was ready, so I was watching for you." She noticed that his breathing was a little heavy. The nurse in her came to the fore. "You don't get enough exercise."

He glanced behind him at the concrete steps. "I just did. Don't you find that a bit much when you come home after a long day?"

"Yes, but I fell in love with the house, stairs and all. Actually, I don't mind them." She shut the door, then gestured behind her.

Brendan saw that in order to get to the living room he had to go up another stairway. "That's fortunate."

She shrugged nonchalantly, leading the way up to the living room. "They keep me in shape."

"And they're doing an excellent job," he murmured to himself as he followed her, his eyes focused on her small waist.

Brendan walked into the living room only to see that the whole condominium had been laid out this way, with small, cozy rooms on each landing. The second level had a kitchen and living room. A cheerfully wallpapered powder room was nestled between landings, with another floor above that. The bedroom, he assumed. The thought brought a prickling of anticipation. He dismissed it, but not easily.

She had done a good job in decorating her home. The rooms he could see were basically done in white, with rose and blue-gray accents. She had accomplished the most with what she had, trying to negate the fact that there was a lot of living space crammed into a small area. The accent was on up instead of out. "Who built this place, a mountain goat?"

Shelby took a half-full bottle of white wine from the refrigerator. She poured the wine into two glasses and laughed as she brought one to him in the living room.

"Yes, but one with excellent taste. My sister Patsy lived here with me until she moved out to get married last year. Fortunately, the mortgage is low."

He accepted the glass mechanically, his attention shifting to her. There were combs in her hair, shimmering green ones. One was nestled on either side, holding her hair away from her face and letting him see the delicate curve of her neck. She was wearing a strapless dark-green-and-white sundress that came in at her waist, then flared out, ending an inch above her knees. The dress was simple. The woman was not. She took his breath away.

Shelby wondered what he was thinking about. The look on his face was pensive. "I thought you might like something other than coffee." She took a sip of her wine. "Where are we going tonight?"

He wanted to stay here. To kiss her and hold her and find out what it would be like to slowly undress her until she stood nude before him, with only the combs in her hair and his warm gaze to adorn her.

"How do you feel about Japanese food?"

There was no hesitation in her answer. Shelby loved food, all types of food. "I love it." The wine made her feel light, airy. The look in his eyes tethered her to earth. And excited her.

Brendan took a long sip of his wine, suddenly needing it. "Then it's lucky I made reservations at a Japanese restaurant."

Shelby moved around a small hassock to get her wrap. As she turned, she was almost standing in his space. "I'm not very difficult to please, Brendan."

She was standing so close to him that when she drew a breath he could almost feel it filling her lungs, feel her breasts brush ever so lightly against him. Another flash of anticipation jolted through him. He could feel a tightening within his stomach, a tightening that was so hard he could hardly draw breath.

Shelby looked at the glass in Brendan's hand and saw his fingertips whiten. "You're going to snap the stem, Brendan."

He looked at her blankly. "What?"

"The glass." She nodded at it. "You're holding on to it so tightly that the stem is going to break."

Chastising himself for his ridiculously adolescent reaction, Brendan placed the glass on the kitchen counter behind Shelby. He had to reach around her to do it. Another bad maneuver.

But he stayed where he was.

"It's probably stress related," he told her. Her eyes looked darker in this light, he thought. More sensuous.

"Probably," she agreed.

"You know what they say about stress, don't you?"

Her breath was feathering along his chin. The tightening within his midsection resumed with a vengeance.

"No, what?" she asked.

He brought her closer to him. "It's better to find a healthy release."

She smiled up at him, waiting. "Are you going to kiss me, Brendan?"

"That's what I was leading up to, yes."

He touched her face with the tips of his fingers, slowly tracing the planes of her face, sensitizing her skin until she almost moaned. And then he lowered his lips to hers in a slow, gentle, probing kiss.

Brendan had no idea that a kiss could feel this way, that it could actually strip him of his senses, of his thoughts, his orientation. It was as if he had just stepped off an airplane to discover that there was nothing beneath his feet—no ramp, no landing, nothing but space. And he was hurtling into it.

Shelby stood on tiptoe, the power of the kiss pulling her up. She anchored her hands on Brendan's arms to keep from falling into the same cavern that he had uncovered for them.

The world outside the kiss ceased to exist.

When their lips parted, her head was spinning. Shelby rested her head against his chest for a moment, trying to get her bearings.

"Wow." She let out a deep, cleansing breath. "Are you sure that's supposed to be the way to reduce stress?"

His laugh, captivated and genuine, rippled beneath her cheek. "No, not anymore."

Shelby raised her head until she looked into his face, her hands still on his chest. "I think we'd better go now."

He glanced toward the upper landing and the room that lay beyond.

"You're right," Brendan said, releasing her. He needed space to compose himself and there was none to be had here. "The reservation's for eight forty-five. They're not very good about holding tables."

Shelby grabbed her clutch purse and slipped her other hand into his. Her shawl was draped across her arm. "All right, let's be on our way."

I had a feeling that we already were, he thought wryly as he held the door open for her.

But he had absolutely no idea where the hell they were going.

Chapter Seven

The restaurant Brendan had selected was charming. She knew it would be. Leading to the entrance was a small wooden bridge that arched elegantly and stretched over a pond stocked with exotic fish that gleamed in the lights from the overhead lanterns like beautiful creatures from another world.

The building was designed to resemble an ancient pagoda. Inside, it was divided into two distinct sections. There was one large, standard dining area with black tables and chairs, its walls covered with colorful silk screenings. The other section of the restaurant consisted of individual private rooms separated from one another by paper walls and sliding doors.

The kimono-clad hostess offered them a choice of dining areas and then waited demurely on the side for their decision.

Brendan turned to Shelby. "Which would you prefer?"

She thought the individual rooms to be far more romantic, but she wanted to see which he would pick. "Why don't you choose? What would *you* like?"

What he would like, he thought, not for the first time, was to kiss her again. To forget about dinner, leave here and explore that wild rush that had overtaken him the moment his lips had touched hers. He wanted to find out if it had been some aberration of nature that would never repeat itself or if lightning could strike again.

The look in his eyes made her warm and Shelby smiled at Brendan, letting him see that she understood and that it was all right.

The decision was not a hard one. He had always preferred privacy. Brendan chose the separate paper-screened room. With a pleased nod, the hostess led them down a small hallway lined with dining rooms, all very discreetly separated from one another.

Brendan took Shelby's arm as he followed the hostess. He glanced at the expression on Shelby's face, one of amused surprised. "What?"

They stopped before the first empty room. "I wouldn't have thought that you would have chosen this." Shelby gestured toward the room.

"Why?"

"Because it's different." Isolated, she added silently. It would be just the two of them, with no distractions or excuses for him to hide behind.

He touched her hair, skimming his fingertips over her cheek. Shelby curbed a desire to press his hand against her skin.

"There's a time to explore and a time to go with the familiar," he answered quietly.

And this, Shelby knew, was a time to explore. For both of them.

Taking hold of his hand for balance, Shelby removed her high heels at the entrance of the small room and placed them neatly by the door.

"Your turn," Shelby urged with a laugh. Brendan placed his hand lightly on her shoulder, then removed his shoes. He lined them up next to hers as if they had always been left this way.

The hostess stood discreetly aside, silently waiting for them to enter first. Shelby stepped in, enchanted by the fairy-tale quality created by the diffused lantern lights that shone through the opaque paper walls. "It's lovely."

Lovely was a word that belonged to her, Brendan thought, watching Shelby. But he said nothing.

Handing them their menus, the hostess backed away, then slid the door closed behind her. They were alone. In the midst of a crowded restaurant, she and Brendan were completely alone.

They looked at each other and smiled slowly. A strange anticipation of things to come filled the air, sending electricity humming between them. Without a word, Brendan took her hand as she began to seat herself at the low table.

"I can manage," she assured him quietly, although she didn't withdraw her hand. She liked the contact, the strength she felt there.

He made no effort to release her hand until she had seated herself on the orange pillow. "Maybe it's just an excuse to hold your hand."

Sitting opposite her, Brendan tucked his legs in beneath him. It wasn't the most comfortable position, but being too comfortable wasn't always a good thing. It caused one to get too sloppy or to go with feelings rather than reason. And right now his reason was slipping. He was experiencing emotions too quickly.

Brendan felt as if he had momentarily lost control of the situation. It was all happening too fast. A sense of foreboding poured over him, and he tried to suppress it. Shelby saw it in his face. She wanted to ask him what was wrong. But she decided that perhaps this was a classic example of discretion being the better part of valor.

Shelby shook her head at his words. "You don't strike me as a person who needs to make excuses to do the things he wants to."

That was the image Brendan portrayed. That was the way he tried to live. But it wasn't completely the truth, he thought.

The atmosphere within the small room was soothing and the evening floated by easily, fortified with good food, soft music and saki that warmed his body almost as much as the nearness of the woman before him. The saki seemed to open up his pores, making him more sensitive to the scent of her perfume, to the sound of her laughter. To her.

Shelby felt deliciously full, but the feeling did not dull her senses the way she might have expected. Instead, every fiber of her body was alert and hungry. Hungry not for food but for more information about the man she was sharing the evening with. She wanted to know everything about him, most especially the secrets that lived in the dark corners of his heart.

"Are you an only child?"

The question surprised him. He had been alone so long that he had never thought of himself as part of anything, certainly not a family that might have siblings.

"As far as I know." He tried to sound casual about his response. The subject of belonging, of family, was not a casual one to him, but she needn't know that.

She had kept away from the subject all evening, but she knew that they couldn't progress any farther in their relationship, if there was to be one, and in her heart she felt that there would be, if she had to skirt around certain matters, leaving them untouched. Small talk only took her so far.

"Then there isn't anyone to take care of your father except for you?"

It had been a beautiful evening and he didn't want to spoil it now by talking about his father. But he should have known better. Shelby was, he was beginning to learn, a woman with a purpose and a very one-track mind at times. If she persisted in this, she was in danger of derailing anything that he thought might have been building between them.

Maybe it was just as well.

His eyes narrowed as he looked at her. "And what am I supposed to do with him?"

She toyed with the tiny cup filled with saki. The liquor had a slightly bitter taste that she found oddly appealing, but only in tiny sips. "What would you like to do with him?"

"Forget he ever existed," Brendan answered with finality. He had no patience with lies, not from others, not from himself. It would have been a lie to tell her that he was happy the man had turned up. With all his heart, he wished Danny hadn't.

Shelby raised her eyes to his. The room was dimly lit, but the emotion within the light green eyes would have been hard for her to miss. "But you can't."

He misunderstood her meaning. He didn't want to be preached to. "Who are you to tell me what I can or can't do?"

"No one." She laid a hand on top of his and felt the extent of his tension. She refused to pull her hand away. "And I'm not telling you. I'm only reading what's in your eyes. Someone once said that eyes are the windows of the soul."

The anger was still there, but at himself, at the old man he couldn't deny no matter how much he felt he should. Brendan laughed shortly. "That would make you a Peeping Tom."

"Maybe."

She lifted her shoulders slightly and then let them drop. Even in his turmoil he wanted to press a kiss to each one, to peel away her dress and lose himself in all her secrets, one by one, until he had lost his ability to think at all.

"Want my advice?" she asked.

He knew that there was no getting away from it. "Is this a trick question?"

Shelby grinned. "No."

He poured a little more saki for himself, wishing that it was something stronger. Brendan wished he could blot out everything from his mind except the sight and scent of the woman he was with. "I have a feeling I'll get it no matter what I say."

Shelby finished the last drop of her saki, savoring it on her tongue, then offered the tiny cup to Brendan to be refilled.

"Then you'd better say yes." She held up her hand before he had filled it halfway. "That's fine." There was only enough in it for another taste, no more. It was all she wanted.

"All right." Brendan placed the bottle back on the small table between them. "What's your advice, oh wise one?"

"Take your father in." She watched his eyes as she said it. They would tell her, more than his words, what he thought of the idea.

He had raised the cup to his lips, and almost choked when he heard her reply. Coughing, he set the cup down and stared at her incredulously. "In to what?"

She leaned over and politely handed him her napkin. "Your home."

"What?"

"From what I've observed, you have very good hearing, Brendan."

He wiped the corner of his mouth. "And you have very bad ideas, Shelby. He's a sick man."

That was not a subject for argument. "He's sick in more ways than one. He's hurt inside."

Brendan handed her back her napkin. "You see that in *his* eyes, I take it."

"Yes." She wasn't daunted by the slight mocking tone in his voice. Shelby sincerely believed in what she was saying. "You would, too, if you weren't so angry at him."

"It's not a good idea." His tone sounded final. He wasn't about to debate this.

"Why?"

Obviously she felt compelled otherwise, he thought. "I'm in court all day. He'd be in the house alone and you said he needed care."

The smile she offered could be termed nothing short of seductive. "Hire a nurse."

He had no idea why the look on her face was so appealing when the subject repelled him this way. "You, I suppose."

Her smile grew wide. "You could do worse."

He fell back on logic and fact, the tools of his trade. "But you work at the hospital."

Shelby shook her head. "Not anymore. I've decided to hand in my resignation. My two older sisters own a private nursing agency. I'm going to be working there."

She was full of surprises. "When?"

"As soon as your father's discharged."

The woman was relentless. "Always go around drumming up business for yourself?" Brendan couldn't help being amused.

Shelby decided that perhaps one more small sip of saki would not be remiss. She offered her cup to him. "If I'm at the right place at the right time, why fight it?"

He filled her cup, then his own before setting down the bottle. "Anyone ever tell you that you're one hell of a pushy lady?"

She welcomed the warmth she felt as the liquor slipped down her throat. "Lots of times."

"What happened?" Even as he tried to resist, he had to admit that the lady fascinated him. Therein lay the danger. But he thought he knew himself well enough to be able to pull back.

"I never listen."

Brendan expected no less. "I didn't think so." He grew serious as he considered her suggestion. There was no getting away from it until they talked it through. "I don't know, Shelby. Taking him in is a big step."

She shook her head, disagreeing. It came as no surprise. He knew she would.

"It's a very small step. The big one is finding it in your heart to forgive him."

Brendan's eyes grew dark as his smile faded completely. "I don't think I can ever do that."

It made her heart cold that he felt that way. There had never been anything but love in her own family. How awful to have lived without it. "Maybe not." She measured her words. "But you'll never know until you give it your best shot."

"Maybe I don't want to give it my best shot." Even as he said it, he didn't know whether he meant it. No, Danny didn't deserve another chance. What he had done was unforgivable.

If Brendan was unsure, Shelby wasn't. She had always believed in the inherent goodness within everyone. "Oh, I think you do."

"Why?" How could she be so sure when he wasn't? Her reasoning eluded him.

She held up two fingers. "One, you wouldn't have come to the hospital to see him if you didn't care somewhere in your heart about what happened to him." She let one finger drop. "Two, you wouldn't have bothered coming to talk to his doctor." Dropping her hand, Shelby waited for his rebuttal.

As a good defensive lawyer, Brendan knew when to retreat from a given line of questioning. She was hitting too close to home and he wasn't ready to let it sink in. He didn't want to feel that he would ever forgive his father. Or that he cared anymore. He was past that.

"You know what?"

Shelby leaned on her upturned hand, her eyes on his, her smile tempting his to join it. "What?"

For a moment he lost his train of thought. She looked beautiful in this light, like a wildflower growing in the meadow, waiting for the warmth of the sun to kiss her. "I think the justice system lost a hell of a lawyer the day you decided to become a nurse."

Shelby took the answer to mean a victory. "Then I'm hired?"

He was lost in the idea of making love with her. Her words caught him off guard. "Excuse me?"

She wanted to laugh at his bewildered expression, but knew she shouldn't. Precious ground would be lost if she did. "Hired," she repeated, then clarified, "As your father's nurse."

That again. He didn't want to commit to that just yet. Maybe there was another way out. "Why don't we see what happens after the surgery tomorrow? Maybe the procedure'll show that something simple is at the base of all his problems." In his heart he knew otherwise. "That and a few meetings at AA and he can go on his way."

He was too intelligent to believe that and they both knew it. But the subject was a raw one and she had pushed it as far as she could for one night.

Shelby set aside her empty cup. "You're right, we'll wait and see."

He wasn't fooled by the complacent expression on her face. "Something tells me you're not too good at waiting." Since she was passing out character judgments so freely, he'd give her one of his own. "You're the type that likes to make things happen."

"Good things," she interjected.

He leaned over and pressed a kiss to her temple. Her skin felt soft, silky. The light scent she wore filled his head, curling out like wispy fingers of smoke through his senses. The kiss was a small, intimate gesture and the fact that he was capable of it took him by surprise. He wasn't one for intimacies. Even making love to a woman had never felt as intimate to him as this small action did. In that single, unguarded moment he had shared a piece of himself, a minute piece, but a piece nonetheless. It was more than he could ever remember doing.

"Very good things," he murmured before he could stop himself. The look in her eyes told him that she understood. Understood, perhaps, more than he did.

"C'mon, Shelby." He rose. "I think I'd better get you home." *Before I make a complete fool of myself.*

The saki was beginning to make her limbs feel heavy. "I think we'd better." She attempted to rise and found she couldn't. "Wait. I'm not sure I can walk. My foot's asleep."

"Is that a direct reflection on my company?" he asked with a smile.

"No, that's a direct reflection on my position for the last two hours. I had my foot tucked under my body." Shelby raised her hand to him.

He took it and helped her to her feet. As she rose and stumbled forward, her leg still numb, her body brushed against him. There was no coyness in the action, nor any self-consciousness, either. She seemed to accept it all as inevitable, their touching, their being together like this. She accepted it far more easily than he did. He was still exploring what it all meant. She acted as if she already knew.

They were quiet for most of the short drive to her home. The music from the radio filled the silence more than adequately and created a dreamy atmosphere.

When they reached her house, Brendan pulled in to the cobblestoned driveway and shut off the engine, but made no move to get out.

She waited a beat, then asked, "Would you care to come in?"

Yes, very much, he thought, but he didn't know if he should. Not just yet. Things were too new, too unpredictable. And carried penalties with them. Penalties that he was more than acquainted with. You care, you hurt. It was as simple as that. And he had had enough of hurting to last a lifetime. "I'm not sure I'm up to mountain climbing."

Brendan knew that it wasn't a good idea to follow through on the feelings he was now experiencing. The intensity was too great and he was afraid of where it might lead. He never went down roads he couldn't see the end of, and this was one that was totally untraveled, at least by him.

She didn't want the evening to end. "The kitchen is on the second level."

"The kitchen?"

"I thought I'd make you a little coffee."

"Coffee again." He turned to look at her. The light from the full moon was infiltrating the interior of the car, outlining her in silver. Brendan ached for her. "We're way past icebreakers, Shelby."

Shelby tilted her face toward his as her fingers lightly touched his cheek. "Yes, I know."

He had no choice. All options were taken out of his hands. It was as if his soul would disintegrate if he didn't kiss her. He leaned over and touched his mouth to hers. The kiss was deliberately light and sweet. It had to be if he was to survive. But even then, it held the promise of things to come. Future things.

One taste of honey still made him ache. He wanted to reach out and hold her, to press her into his arms, against his body. To absorb her until he didn't know where he ended and she began. He wanted a myriad of things he had never even thought about until this moment. It had all been out of reach for him before, beginning with the physical closeness.

It still was.

"Bucket seats do not promote intimacy," he said lightly, releasing her.

She wasn't fooled by his tone. His heart was racing just like hers. She had felt it beneath her hand as she had placed it on his chest.

"Maybe it's better that there is a little time out." She did her best to regulate her breathing. "Will you be at the hospital tomorrow morning?"

"I have to be in court." And if he hadn't, he would have found another excuse to use.

She accepted his answer without probing, even though she felt he was hiding behind the excuse. "I'll call you, then, when it's over."

She had told him that her regular shift was from nine to three. "You're on the morning shift again?"

"No." She laughed lightly. "Nurses are allowed on the floor even when they're not on duty."

"I don't understand, Shelby." Why was she putting herself out like this? Danny Connery couldn't possibly mean anything to her. And Brendan refused to have the old man mean anything to him. He was just a stranger with the same last name. Why, then, was she doing all this? Why was she getting so involved?

She saw the question in his eyes, saw the hurt he fought to keep back each time they mentioned his father. "No, I'm sure you don't. But I hope you will. Soon."

She leaned over again and just lightly touched her lips to his. "I'll see you tomorrow." It wasn't a question. It was a given.

Shelby moved back in her seat and fished out her key. "I'll see myself to the door." She turned to look at him one last time. "I had a wonderful evening, Brendan. Thank you."

And with that she got out of the car and hurried up the stairs to her front door.

Brendan sat in his car watching her until she was safely inside the house. There was too much to think about. Thoughts crowding his mind, he forced himself to blank out everything.

It was better that way, at least for now.

Chapter Eight

Her alarm clock was set for 5:00 a.m., but Shelby was awake before it rang. An inner clock that was far more finely tuned went off inside her head ten minutes before the electrical one did.

Half-asleep, Shelby forced herself to get up. She groped around the perimeter of her bed, tucking in the blue-and-white comforter as best she could in her groggy state, striving for some semblance of neatness. She absolutely hated coming home to an unmade bed. Spontaneous by nature, Shelby still possessed a deep-seated love of order.

Within twenty minutes, fortified by an extra-strong cup of coffee, Shelby was dressed and in her car, driving toward the hospital some fifteen miles from her home. She wasn't due in until nine. The nursing complement on her floor was back up to a healthy number again, emphasis on the word *healthy,* she thought. And by all rights, she could have slept in until at least six o'clock, if not seven.

But Brendan's father was due in surgery at seven-thirty. And he needed someone to hold his hand. Shelby knew that Brendan wouldn't be there. She doubted if he had to be in court anywhere near the time of the surgery, but she knew that whatever there was between the two men would keep him from coming. Even if he wanted to. She firmly believed that he did, though he might not know it yet.

Maybe, she thought as she made a careful left turn into the hospital parking lot, she *had* to believe that Brendan wanted to be there, that he cared. She would never allow herself to become involved with a callous man. And she was involved.

No, it wasn't just wishful thinking on her part. She knew. Brendan did care. The problem was, for whatever reasons he harbored, he just didn't want to and fought against it.

Cindy, the newest nurse on the floor, looked up in surprise when Shelby walked into the nurses' station. "What are you doing here?"

"Is that any way to greet a dedicated nurse?" Shelby stashed her purse in the drawer of the desk she would use during the next shift.

"I would have thought that the dedicated nurse would have been sleeping," Soo-ling said, walking up behind her. "You are behind by twenty-six hours, so you told me the other day."

Shelby turned when she heard Soo-ling's soft voice. "I can catch up later. Mr. Connery's due in surgery this morning."

Anna, the nurse who took care of Danny during the early shift, looked up from her notes at the mention of the man's name.

"It's only a simple procedure, Shelby." She cocked her head and moved her wide-framed glasses back up the bridge of her long, narrow nose. "Personal interest?"

Shelby nodded. "You might say that."

Anna checked her watch. "Well then, you'd better hurry if you want to see him. They're going to take him to pre-op at six."

Shelby nodded. She knew the routine in her sleep. An hour or so before an operation, patients were taken down to pre-op, an area near the operating rooms. There, they were prepared and properly medicated to insure that everything went smoothly.

But fear was something there was no medication for. At least, not in the lasting sense, she mused. It was probably something that Danny had come to discover as alcohol had brought him to his knees. Turning around, she headed for his room.

"Good morning, Mr. Connery." She walked in and left the door open behind her.

Danny's tired, pale face seemed to come to life at the very sight of Shelby.

"Hello, Shelly-girl." He tried to sit up, but the medication he had received fifteen minutes earlier was beginning to make his limbs feel even heavier than they already felt.

He squinted at her, trying to focus his eyes and his mind, already groggy. "What are you doing here? Is it nine already? Did they forget about me?" The words were uttered wistfully. There was no clock in the room and he wore no wristwatch.

Shelby shook her head. "No, they didn't forget about you. I thought I'd come by and hold your hand for a few minutes before they take you down to pre-op."

Picking up his hand, she found that it was ice-cold. Without a word, she slipped one of his hands between both of her own, trying to warm him.

"There's nothing to it," she promised gently. "Like falling off a log."

"I've done my share of that in my time," Danny said with a dry laugh.

The laugh turned into a rasping cough. Shelby reached for the ice pitcher, then stopped. Danny was to have no liquids before his surgery. If he did, surgery would be rescheduled for another day. Helpless, Shelby stood by, holding his hand tightly and waiting until he caught his breath again.

His eyes redder than usual, Danny looked a bit chagrined as he asked Shelby, "Um, is my son..." He couldn't finish the question.

She couldn't stand to see the last shreds of his pride crumble this way. "No, that's what I'm doing here. He asked me to call him right after surgery's over. He's due in court early this morning and—"

Danny waved away her explanation. She wondered if he knew that she was making part of it up. If he did, he was letting them both have the safety of the lie.

"Proud of him, I am." His voice faded in and out as he spoke. "He did it all on his own. No help from me. No help at all."

He blinked, trying to make out her face. His vision was becoming fuzzy, more so than usual. "I left him, you know. Him and his mother."

Shelby's heart quickened. So *that* was why. It explained a great deal. "No, I didn't know."

"I did." Even with the medication slowly making him more and more disoriented, the shame rose up like gall in his mouth, choking him. "Couldn't face responsibility. Partyin', that's all I was ever good for."

A tear of regret trickled out of the corner of his eye, falling down his face in a zigzag pattern until it became a tiny wet spot on the pillow right next to his face.

"I left him and his mother when he was just a boy. Left them because I had no courage." He moved his head from side to side, as if that would erase the pain. But it didn't. "No good, I was no good."

Shelby took his hand again and squeezed it. "Don't say that. Brendan's mother—"

"Delia." He uttered the woman's name as reverently as if it was a prayer.

"Delia," Shelby repeated. "She wouldn't have married you if she had thought that you were no good." The hopeless expression remained imprinted on his face. Shelby thought quickly. "Brendan wouldn't have brought you here if he hadn't thought you were worthwhile."

The reddened, glazed eyes, filled with tears, looked at her, wanting so hard to believe, to take comfort in the smallest shred. "You think so?"

"I don't think. I know." She looked down at him, her smile encouraging.

"Bless you," he mumbled. His eyes were growing incredibly heavy as everything else began to float away. "You'll be good for him, you will," he murmured, as if to himself. "Stay with Danny." It was a plea. "He needs someone."

"I'll stay with you," she promised.

Shelby heard a commotion behind her and turned to see Anna and an orderly entering the room. Between them they were guiding a gurney.

"Your magic carpet's here, Mr. Connery," Anna announced as Shelby stepped out of the way. The orderly moved the orange chair aside and lined up the gurney next to the bed.

Danny still clutched Shelby's hand in his. Suddenly a wave of anxiety set in. "Shelly?"

Shelby bent over him. "I'm here." She saw the fear flaming in his eyes, felt the panic in his grip. She made a decision. "I'm going down with him, Anna. You can stay here."

Anna shrugged. "As long as there's a nurse with him, makes no difference to me. There's plenty of work up here to keep me busy from now until Christmas."

Shelby laughed. "Don't I know it." She flashed the older woman a smile of gratitude.

Shelby helped the orderly transfer Danny from the stationary bed onto the gurney. She was amazed at how fragile the old man felt. She guessed that in his time he must have been a bull of a man. His weight, according to the medical chart, was down to a hundred and twenty pounds. His large-boned frame made him look as if it was even less than that.

The exploratory procedure normally took a little more than an hour and a half, counting the down time when a patient was being put under and then brought out again from the anesthetic. Shelby stayed outside the operating room the entire time, foregoing the regular waiting room that lay just beyond. She was much too keyed up to sit calmly and wait.

When Dr. Hemsley came out through the swinging doors of the operating room, his green operating gown flapping loosely about his green-trousered legs, Shelby was quick to accost him.

"Dr. Hemsley." The man turned to his right at the sound of his name. "How did it go?"

"Are you the next of kin now..." He paused a minute, obviously trying to recall her name. "Shelby?" There was no censure in his manner, only vague curiosity as to her involvement with the patient.

"I'm standing in for Mr. Connery's son," she explained quickly. "He wanted me to call him as soon as the operation was over."

Hemsley pulled off his cap and removed the ends of his mask. "All right. Saves me the trouble of calling." He gestured her toward the waiting room. "Do you mind? I've been on my feet since four-thirty."

Shelby preceded him into the waiting room and took a seat on the nearest sofa. The surgeon dropped down next to her, sighing. She didn't know if it was because he was tired or because the news was difficult to deliver. She fervently hoped for the former.

"Surprisingly enough," the doctor began, "the man does not have cirrhosis of the liver. There's some damage, of course, but nothing he couldn't live with as long as he gave up drinking."

He was being purposely evasive. "What did the laparoscopy show?" she pressed.

He paused, as if weighing something in his mind. "It's as I suspected, actually. His entire body is worn down by years of neglect and abuse. But that, I'm afraid, is not the problem."

Shelby held her breath. "What is?"

But the doctor wouldn't be pinned down yet. "I had an MRI done on him late yesterday afternoon. I'm waiting for the final report. It should be in my office this afternoon. The preliminary one wasn't hopeful, but I don't want to alarm the family until I'm certain." He looked at her and his meaning was clear. "I'm calling in Dr. Jacobs. Henry Jacobs."

There were two doctors named Jacobs associated with the hospital. Henry Jacobs was a top neurosurgeon. "Then the problem is neurological?" she asked.

Again he paused, as if wondering if he should voice his suspicions to her. She realized that the concern in her face must have won him over. Suddenly Shelby thought that he looked years older as he uttered the words that were a death sentence for some. "I think it's a brain tumor."

Shelby caught her breath. "Then the blurred vision, the headaches—"

He nodded his head in agreement with her unspoken conclusion. "It wasn't just due to the alcohol, no."

A brain tumor. The waiting area suddenly felt cold to her. "Is it operable?"

There were no false words of comfort. "That's what the report will tell me." He rose again, moving like a man with a heavy burden. "I don't want the family..."

Shelby rose with him. "There's only his son," she put in, feeling oddly hollow, disjointed. How was Brendan going to take this newest curve that fate had thrown him? And what of Danny? Did he suspect?

Dr. Hemsley nodded. "I'd rather not have him know until I have all the information at my disposal. No need in alarming him yet."

"I understand." She let out a long breath. It didn't help. "Thank you for telling me."

She turned to go. She had to call Brendan. She had told him she would. He'd be suspicious if she didn't. How was she going to keep this out of her voice?

"Shelby," the doctor called after her.

She turned and looked at him. "Yes?"

He took the few steps toward her and surprised her by putting an arm around her shoulders. It was a fatherly gesture. "Mind taking a bit of advice from an old man who's been around?"

Normally she would have protested something about his not being old at all. But she was too numb to rise to the occasion. Her mind was on Danny. And on Brendan. "Yes, Doctor?"

"Don't get involved. I knew a very good nurse once." He looked at her as if he was picturing the woman again. "You remind me of her a little. She got involved with almost every patient she came in contact with. They all loved her. But she gave bits and pieces of herself away until there was nothing left. And then when one of her patients died, it almost destroyed her." He dropped his hand and looked at her squarely. "You can't help if you cry, Shelby."

"I'll try to remember that." But Shelby believed that she could.

The phone on his desk rang at nine-fifteen. Brendan realized that he had been watching the clock, waiting for her call. His mind was supposed to be on the Hudson case. It was coming up for trial. He had just ordered several subpoenas sent out, but it had taken him longer than usual to get things organized. To get himself organized. He was preoccupied by the drama playing itself out in the hospital. And by the memory of a flame-haired woman he had held briefly in his arms.

Brendan was waiting for her call. Waiting to hear the sound of her low, melodic voice tell him that it was going to be all right. That the man he swore he didn't care about was nothing more than the con artist he had taken him for and that there was nothing wrong with him that drink and time hadn't accomplished. And could undo.

And he was waiting for the sound of her voice because it had been floating through his brain all night, all morning, and he wanted it to solidify. To hear the texture, the softness.

He jabbed the intercom button. "Mr. Connery," Rita said, "it's a Miss Tyree on line three."

He looked down at the flashing red light on the streamlined black telephone. "I'll take it." He pushed the button down, and the flashing ceased.

"Brendan?" Her breathless voice floated through the receiver. She was making the call from one of the many public telephones located on the hospital's main floor. She'd chosen a phone booth for privacy. "This is Shelby. Your dad's in recovery right now."

He dragged his hand through his hair as he sat back in his chair. "What did they find?"

She wanted to tell him, tell him everything, to share this awful suspicion that the doctor had. To share the burden of knowing, of fearing.

But she refrained. Hemsley had looked at the preliminary photographs. Maybe he had misinterpreted them. It wouldn't have been the first time an initial reading was incorrect. After all, that was why there were specialists to read and do the reports. There was absolutely no reason to drop this on Brendan until she was certain it was true.

"Nothing, really, just confirming some of Dr. Hemsley's initial impressions. There's some damage to the liver. Some signs of angina and hardening of the arteries, but that's to be expected."

Brendan wasn't fooled. "What's the bad news, Shelby?" He could hear the hesitation in her voice. Brendan was used to picking up small nuances, little telltale inflections in witnesses' voices. He knew something was wrong.

With effort, she forced herself to sound cheerful. "There isn't any—yet," she added, hoping that would put him off. "Dr. Hemsley wants to do more tests."

"I see." He saw more than she was telling him. Not wanting to really know, uncertain as to how he would react to anything serious, Brendan let the matter drop for the time being.

She was relieved that he wasn't pressing her for more information. She didn't know if she could continue to lie to him. "Will you be by to see him this afternoon? He should be back in his room before noon."

His schedule was in front of him on his desk, but he didn't look at it. He knew it by heart. He always did. "I'm in court."

Shelby pressed her lips together. He was being stubborn. "This evening, then?"

He didn't want to go back to the hospital. Each time he did, the trap grew tighter. He didn't want the jaws to snap closed on him. He wanted to keep distance between himself and the man who called himself his father.

"Perhaps."

Why did he have to be like this? Why couldn't he open his heart? Danny was obviously needy. She knew that if Brendan refused, there would be no hope for them, either. And she wanted there to be.

But right now her main concern was for Danny, and for the pain that Brendan was letting fester in his heart.

"I think you should come. When do you think you'll be through in court?"

Her relentlessness never ceased to amaze him. He had never known anyone with such persistence. "Five o'clock, probably."

"I could meet you here if you wanted some moral support when you see him."

"Shelby—" there was an exasperated edge to his voice "—I don't need moral support." *I need to be left alone.*

The tension she felt in harboring the doctor's confidence broke through, heating her impatience with his stubbornness. "Well, you certainly need something. He's your father, Brendan."

He turned in his chair, looking out on the view from his third-story office window. There were storm clouds gathering in the distance, turning the afternoon gray. "He didn't remember that. Why should I?"

She wanted to tell him that she knew about his past, that Danny had told her about walking out on him and his mother. That she understood his pain and wanted to help him heal. But above all, she wanted Brendan to volunteer that information to her himself. She wanted him to trust her enough to tell her.

"He's proud of you, Brendan. He told me that today. Very proud." Everyone wanted their parents to be proud of them, no matter how much they denied it. There was a small child still within every adult that hungered for that sort of approval.

"Shelby..." Brendan began, then sighed. What was the use? The woman would go down arguing, and he was already tired. He lifted his briefcase from the floor and placed it on his desk.

She shifted in the phone booth, bracing herself for more of the same. "What?"

"Never mind." He gave up. Maybe he really wanted to be persuaded and was letting her do it. He didn't know anymore. This was turning him inside out. "I'll be there at six."

She felt a wave of relief. "Fine. I'll meet you at the nurses' station."

He was naturally distrustful and still didn't understand her interest. It went above and beyond nursing. "Don't you have a life of your own to lead?"

"Yes, and I'm leading it." If his words stung, she wasn't about to show him. "This is what I choose to do, Brendan."

He couldn't resist. Even now she was getting to him. "Nag people?"

She heard the slight smile in his voice and responded in kind. "Prod consciences," she corrected.

Brendan slid his notes into his briefcase and snapped it closed, cradling the phone against his neck with his shoulder. "Jiminy Cricket was green," he reminded her.

Shelby laughed, suddenly feeling light. Another minor battle won. He was coming along. "We all have handicaps to work with."

"Yes." Brendan thought of the hole his father had burned in his emotions, in his ability to reach out without fear. Danny Connery had completely demolished his ability to love. "We all have handicaps."

Shelby knew by the tone of Brendan's voice that they weren't talking about a sweet fairy tale any longer. They were talking about the scars Danny Connery had left upon his only son's soul. Scars she was determined to heal.

Chapter Nine

Shelby pushed the heavy swinging doors apart slowly and entered. The doors silently closed behind her as her eyes traveled the length of the room.

It wasn't what she had expected.

It didn't look like the courtroom she had seen on television or in the movies. It seemed smaller somehow, yet intimidating. It was as if there could be no secrets hidden here.

The jury box was empty, as was the courtroom. Only an hour earlier there had been an indictment held here. Shelby approached the jury box and ran her hand along the long railing, trying to absorb the solemnness of the room. This was where Brendan worked. Where he spoke and pleaded other people's cases.

No, *pleaded* was not the right word, she decided. Shelby couldn't see Brendan pleading, not for any reason. Not because he didn't care but because words like that would not come to him. He was too controlled to beg or plead. He merely presented facts.

Shelby's thoughts turned to yesterday, to the kiss that had taken them both by such surprise. Maybe he wasn't entirely too controlled, she amended mentally, a smile playing on her lips.

"Slumming?"

She whirled around, surprised to see Brendan behind her even though she had come here looking for him. His dark brows were raised in question as he set his brief-case down on the long defense table. His business finished, he had seen her quite by chance when he glanced through the small windows into the room. He had been on his way out.

"What are you doing here?" She had said she'd meet him at the hospital. Had something gone wrong after all? He told himself that it didn't matter to him if it had.

Shelby tried to read his expression and couldn't. Was he angry with her for coming here, where he worked? "I called your office. Your secretary told me that I'd find you here."

He had been thinking of her all morning, during his briefing with the judge, during his interview with his client. While he had been stuck in traffic on his way to the courthouse. In very little time she had managed to infiltrate the inner workings of his mind. It wasn't a good sign. Neither was the fact that he was so pleased to see her.

"And you managed to track me down?" The court-house was big and easy to get lost in, yet she had found him.

Shelby relaxed a little. His tone had lost some of its defensive edge. "She was very helpful. She gave me the number of the courtroom."

"How did you manage to get that out of Rita?" His secretary was nothing if not closemouthed when it came to dealing with people who called the office. It was only those within her chosen inner circle that received the benefit of her mothering nature. To anyone else, Rita McClay was the soul of professional aloofness, offering only as much information as she had been authorized to give.

Shelby shrugged, wondering what the mystery was. The woman had been perfectly nice to her. "I told her who I was."

Brendan leaned his elbow on the jury-box railing and looked at her, as if trying to discern the answer to that question himself.

"And just who are you?" *Who are you and why are you in my life now, at this moment, when everything else seems to be coming apart?*

Shelby saw the torment in his eyes a moment before he managed to lock it away. "Your father's nurse," she answered simply. "Your friend, if you need one."

No, it wouldn't be his friend she'd become if he let her. She'd be his deliverance. And his undoing.

"I'm not in the market for a friend, Shelby."

She wanted to reach out and soothe him, to make the hurt that he carried around with him go away. She didn't know how. Shelby kept talking, hoping to grope her way to something that would make a difference.

"It's not something you can find in a market," she said quietly. "It's someone who just happens along when you least expect it."

He watched her as she crossed to the area separating the spectators from the vital players in each courtroom drama. "Why are you here, Shelby?"

His voice was low and there was a guarded edge to it again. Was she crowding him? Or was there something else wrong?

She turned to face him. "I thought perhaps you'd need a little moral support before you got to the hospital."

Now it was clear. Unconsciously he relaxed a little. She wasn't going to tell him anything he didn't want to hear. No news from the hospital. "Translation, you didn't think I would go on my own."

Shelby smiled. So much for euphemisms. "The thought did cross my mind."

He picked up his attaché case from the table where he had left it. "I don't run from things, Shelby. That's my father's role."

She hadn't meant to open wounds again. She wanted only to help them heal. "Fine," she said brightly, hooking her arm through his, "then I'll buy you a quick dinner before we go to the hospital."

He found himself laughing. "Is food the way you soothe everything?"

A bailiff walked in through the rear entrance and looked at them quizzically. Brendan recognized him and nodded. The bailiff had been in court earlier when he had been closeted with Judge Anderson.

Shelby smiled at the bailiff as he passed. Brendan wondered if she smiled at everyone. Probably.

"No, not everything," she answered. "But it's a good second."

Brendan held the swinging gate open for her. "What's the first?"

"Listening," she told him as she stepped through.

He followed her out of the courtroom. "That's when someone has something to say."

"Everyone has something to say." She stopped in the long, sterile hallway to look at him. It was getting late and most of the people had already gone home for the day. "Some people just have trouble saying it, that's all."

"You certainly don't." He placed his hand on the small of her back and guided her toward the front of the building.

She liked the feel of his hand on her. "No, fortunately, I've never had that problem."

"Fortunate for whom?"

"Me." Shelby looked over her shoulder back at the courtroom they had just left. "Can I come watch you work sometime?"

The note of genuine interest in her voice amused him. "It's not like a floor show, Shelby."

"I know that." They resumed walking, their footsteps echoing before them down the hall. "I was just curious what you were like in court. Whether I'd see a vein of passion spring up when you make your final statement before the jury. Did I get that right?" She cast a side-glance in his direction. "Final statement?"

He wanted to kiss her. She looked so pure, so clean. So tempting. But criminal lawyers weren't supposed to give in to temptation. At least, he wasn't. "Yes." He laughed. "That's what it's called."

They came to a staircase. Since they were on the second floor and he preferred walking, Brendan offered Shelby a choice. "Stairs or elevator?" He indicated the flight before them.

"You must be kidding. Stairs, of course." She placed her hand on the wooden railing. "I don't know much about being a lawyer," she admitted. "This was my first time in a courtroom."

Courtrooms had been so much a part of his life for the past seven years he couldn't imagine not being familiar with them. "Never had a ticket?"

"Nope." Her expression was smug. "Not a one."

"Very commendable."

"Very lucky," she corrected. Shelby came to the landing and looked down. The courthouse foyer below was wide and all encompassing, as if gathering everyone in its arms before sending them on into rooms to await their fate. "It wasn't as big as I thought it'd be. The courtroom, I mean."

She went down the remaining stairs, then turned and waited as he caught up. "What did you do here today? Did you have a case?"

He had no idea why it was so pleasant to talk to her about his day. He only knew that it was. Brendan wasn't used to anyone asking about his day or wanting to know. "I had to see the presiding judge in his chambers."

Shelby thought that over and came to no conclusion. "Is that good?"

He smiled at her question. "Neither good nor bad. Just going over a few preliminary things with the judge and the D.A."

She thought of the courtroom drama she had seen. "Sounds exciting."

Brendan shook his head. "On the contrary, very cut-and-dried."

Shelby turned her face up to his. They were suddenly only inches apart. "Excitement, counselor, is what you make it."

Her mouth was tempting him. Its sweetness suddenly echoed through his system, reminding him, making him crave more. He forgot where he was. He forgot who he was. With a hand against her slender throat, his fingers caressing the soft skin he found there, Brendan brushed his lips against hers.

He should have known better. He couldn't just kiss this woman and go on with his life as if nothing had happened. His life, each time he kissed her, ceased to exist. Everything ceased but the mad pounding of his blood in his ears and the intense desire that pulsated through his body, making him ache for her so badly that he couldn't think straight. He couldn't think at all.

He pulled her into his arms, deepening the kiss until they were both breathless.

Each time it was better. The touch of his lips to hers brought a thrill she couldn't begin to put into words. It made her soul sing. It was special, wonderful, and she was going to see to it that he felt the same way about it that she did.

"See?" she asked, a smile spreading as her lips drew away. "Excitement *is* what you make it."

To his surprise, he was smiling as well. *No*, he thought, *excitement is you.*

He realized that the guard at the front entrance was watching them intently. Brendan didn't care to be someone's source of entertainment.

"You promised me a quick supper," Brendan said to Shelby as he gathered his senses to him.

Shelby had noticed the guard, too, but unlike Brendan the thought of someone watching them didn't bother her. Only Brendan's reticence did that.

"And I'm a woman of my word." Shelby linked her arm through his. "Let's go, counselor. Unless, of course, you have to consult with the judge again."

He shook his head. "I'm through consulting people for the day. You found me just as I was getting ready to leave."

"That makes me lucky."

She sounded as if she meant it. Brendan hadn't the slightest clue as to why.

Brendan followed Shelby to a table, a tray holding a cheeseburger, fries and soda in his hands. The French fries were spilling out and over the cheeseburger. "This is what you mean by dinner?"

Shelby placed her tray on the only available table and slid in. The table seated two. Just barely.

"This is what I mean by quick." She pushed a straw through the top of her drink container. "Besides, all these people can't be wrong."

He watched in bemused fascination as she dabbed a thin red line of ketchup on her fries. "Why not? It's been known to happen. Look at world wars."

He must be one heck of a lawyer, she thought. He found a way to argue over everything. "Do you always approach things so negatively?"

"Occupational habit. If you start from a negative angle, it can't get any worse. And maybe it can improve."

Ignoring his fries, Brendan tackled the double-deck cheeseburger that Shelby had foisted on him. Tiny bits of lettuce rained down on either side as he bit into it.

She wondered if he meant that. She supposed it had some merit. "Well, at least there's a hope for you, then. You should eat your French fries," she pointed out, "before they get cold."

Brendan couldn't remember when he had last been to one of these fast-food places. The closest he had come to one was ordering roast beef sandwiches from a local deli when he was working late at the office.

He glanced at the red container overflowing with thin sticks of fries, but didn't pick one up. "I don't like French fries."

Her own finished, Shelby commandeered his fries from his tray. "I'm not sure, but I think that's un-American." He laughed at her nonsensical quip and his reaction pleased her. "Feel better?"

Actually, he did. Being with her seemed to accomplish that. "About what?"

She gestured in the air, a French fry still in her fingers. "Everything. You don't look as tense as you did in the courtroom."

He looked around. All the other tables were occupied. Several lines snaked their way to the front counter as people waited their turn to order. The din swelled and engulfed them so that he had to raise his voice to be heard.

"Eating in a noisy place with whining children and harried mothers pushing strollers has a strange sort of soothing effect."

Shelby grinned at his comment. "Knew you'd see it my way." Brendan merely shook his head.

She waited until she had finished her hamburger before she launched into another frontal assault. "Dr. Hemsley said he'd be at the hospital around seven tonight, making his rounds again." She raised her eyes to his hopefully. "I thought..."

By now he knew how her mind worked. Funny how that had happened so quickly. He usually kept his distance from people. He couldn't with her. The circumstances seemed to be beyond his control.

"That I'd want to talk to him," Brendan concluded for her.

Shelby watched a woman with a double stroller maneuver her way between tables, trying to get out. "At least to him."

She never stopped, he thought. She'd go on until she wore his resistance down. "Meaning?"

Shelby played with the straw, twirling it around in the ice. "Well, your father is there, too."

He was through with his meal. Through with a lot of things, or so he thought. "I know that."

Shelby backed off a little and dropped her eyes. "Just mentioning it."

It made him laugh again. Though he resisted at every turn, she was making things like laughter easier for him. The danger was in getting used to it.

"You do that well." When she looked at him quizzically, he elaborated. "Mention things."

She interpreted that as a truce. "Have I mentioned that I'm quitting Harris Memorial and joining my sister's nursing agency?"

"Yes, you did. Several times."

She took a deep breath, waiting. "And?"

"And?" he echoed.

"Brendan." Shelby put her hand on his. She didn't have to say any more.

The woman at the next table had three children under the age of five with her and was trying her best to conduct what passed for a sane meal. A French fry went flying overhead, passing Shelby. The mother cried out the child's name sharply, then smiled apologetically at Shelby.

But Shelby's attention was not on flying French fries. It was on Brendan.

He didn't know what to say to her. He didn't want to take his father in. To bring him in would be to reopen old wounds even wider than they already were. "Shelby, you're asking more of me than I can give."

The harried woman gathered her brood together and rose. "Listen to him, honey," she said, stopping by Shelby. "When they say they can't commit, believe them. Mine said it and he left me with these." She sighed as she shepherded her children out.

Brendan made an impatient sound as he tried again. "My father—"

Shelby leaned forward. "Yes?"

A tray crashed and a child started screaming simultaneously. Brendan gave up.

"I don't think this place is the right atmosphere for this conversation." He took her tray and dumped its contents on his, then stacked the trays together. He rose, the trays in his hands. "There *is* no right atmosphere for this conversation." He marched out, depositing the trays on his way.

Shelby hurried after him to the parking lot where they had left their cars. Perforce, they had arrived separately. "I thought you said you never ran from responsibilities."

Brendan turned to face her, his eyes cold. Shelby gathered her courage to her and pressed on, for all three of their sakes. He had to open up, had to forgive. Nothing else had a chance of growing if he didn't clear away the nettles of anger that were festering there now.

"He's your responsibility, Brendan." She placed her hand on his arm. "You can't just forget about him and leave him somewhere. Without you, he'll curl up and die."

He shook off her hand. "What do you know about it?" What gave her the right to dictate terms? She didn't know, couldn't know, what he had gone through.

The look in his eyes was like a physical blow. But Shelby rallied. "I know enough, have seen enough, to put together pieces. Brendan, you won't be able to face yourself if you abandon him now."

The pain he had kept buried for so long surfaced, overflowing. "He did. He abandoned us."

Didn't he see? "And you'll become what he became. Perhaps the Armani suits'll still be in place and there'll be no white stubble. But emotionally—" she pleaded for him to open his mind "—Brendan, emotionally you'll be as empty, as bereft as that old man is."

He turned to walk to his car, fighting to keep from telling her things he could never take back once they were said.

"I already am." He opened his door.

Shelby pushed it closed again, turning so that he was forced to face her. "No, you are not," she insisted. "Not yet."

He could have pushed her out of the way. He was certainly strong enough to. Part of him wanted to, wanted to get away from her, from what she was saying. But part of him wanted to be convinced.

He stayed where he was. "What makes you think that?"

An inch. She was winning by an inch. It was up to her to stretch that. Shelby sagged against his car, momentarily drained.

"Instincts. You're not the man your father was. You won't turn your back when someone needs you." She believed that with all her heart. Believed in him the way he wouldn't in himself.

Brendan lowered his voice. They were attracting attention. "Why is it that you think you know me so well?" She had no basis for it. He had ceased wondering why she was concerning herself with all this. He had accepted it as her way. But the rest, the rest needed explaining.

"I just do." She tilted her head back to see him better. "Sometimes words aren't necessary."

A car pulled up behind them, trying to angle into the spot next to Brendan's car. Brendan stepped aside, taking Shelby with him.

He sighed, relenting. How could he have thought there would be another conclusion drawn? "I suppose I can take him in, until he gets back on his feet."

Shelby rose and kissed Brendan on the cheek. "It's a start."

"It's everything," he said with a finality she couldn't argue with. The small spot her lips had touched felt alive and warm. The rest of him felt cold. He didn't want his father living with him, didn't want to see the old man on a regular basis. He didn't want to set himself up again for a fall. Loving and believing once had been enough.

She wanted to hear him repeat it. "And you'll take him in when he's released?"

"Yes, I'll take him in after he's released."

She threaded her arms through his. "Fine, I'll tell Irene."

He felt the soft impression of her breasts and tried not to react. He might as well have tried not to breathe for all the good it did him. "Irene?"

"My sister."

"Why?" he asked sarcastically. "Is she posting it on the evening news?"

His tone didn't bother her. She saw through him by now. "No, but she runs the agency. She'll make the arrangements."

The way she had talked, he had imagined Shelby run
ning everything. "I thought you were doing all that."

"No, I can't usurp her."

A smile quirked his lips. "Why not? You've certainly
usurped me."

She looked up at him solemnly. "Not without you:
permission."

Brendan didn't know what to make of her. "I've neve:
known anyone who professed to know me better than
know myself." He walked her to her car.

She fished out her car keys, then unlocked the ca:
door. She looked at Brendan over her shoulder. "Maybe
you just haven't looked deeply enough into yourself."

He had never wanted to look deep. That was why he
had buried himself so well in his work. It left no time fo:
introspection, for feeling and mourning over losses.

Brendan followed her in his car to the hospital, mar
veling at how naturally he had allowed himself to be led
It seemed to him that she was leading him around a lo
these past few days. He had to do something about tha
and soon before things got too out of hand.

If they hadn't already.

They parked on the second level of visitors' parking
and took the familiar route to the elevators in the back
of the east wing. The elevator arrived on the fifth floo:
without stopping on any other floor.

With evening setting in, the floor had a subdued
quality about it. The dinner hour over, the pace had
settled down to a more leisurely one.

Shelby smiled and nodded a greeting to one of the
nurses. "Is Dr. Hemsley here yet?"

The nurse responded affirmatively and pointed. "He's
in with the patient in 536 now."

That was Danny's room. Just in time. "Let's go," Shelby urged.

But the tension had returned. "I'll wait outside until he's finished," Brendan told her.

Shelby looked toward the closed door, torn. But of the two, Brendan needed her more. "Okay," she agreed. "We both will."

The doctor emerged from the room within a few minutes. His frown was pensive as he stepped out into the hall. He didn't see them at first and almost walked right by.

"Doctor?" Shelby stopped him.

Brendan hung back, a premonition preventing him from asking anything. He was annoyed at himself for what he felt was his own cowardice. He had repeatedly told himself that the old man didn't mean anything to him. Why, then, was there fear?

"Oh, Mr. Connery." The doctor turned, seeing them for the first time. "I was going to call you. I'd like to have a word with you about your father."

The tone was not promising. Shelby placed her hand on Brendan's arm, but he hardly seemed to notice. His expression was stoic as he looked at the doctor. "Yes?"

The doctor waved them over to the side, away from Danny's door. "I went over the final results of the MRI this afternoon."

"MRI?" Brendan looked at Shelby for an explanation but it was the doctor who answered.

"It's a series of intensified photographs of a part of the body. In your father's case, his brain." Dr. Hemsley paused, not for dramatic significance but because the words seemed hard to say. "I'm afraid the news is not good."

"What is it?" Brendan expected the numbness he felt regarding his father to continue. He had no idea why a sudden flash of anxiety would grip him. Unconsciously he took Shelby's hand.

"He has a brain tumor."

Brendan squeezed Shelby's hand tightly. "What are the odds involved in surgery?"

The doctor slowly moved his head from side to side. "Surgery of this nature is always a very risky proposition, Mr. Connery."

Brendan picked up the unspoken word in the doctor's voice. "But?"

Dr. Hemsley squared his shoulders beneath his shapeless houndstooth-check jacket, as if that might help him carry the burden of having to say what he was about to say. "But in this case, I'm afraid it's inoperable. The tumor is embedded in such a way that it can't successfully be reached and removed."

Shelby drew in her breath. There was nothing she could say. She could only be there for him.

"Does he know?" Brendan wanted to know.

"No, I haven't told him yet. I—"

If asked, Brendan couldn't have said what he was feeling at the moment. Or if he even could feel. "How long does he have?"

The doctor shook his head. "I honestly don't know. Six months. Six years. These things have a way of surprising us sometimes." He tried to sound encouraging. "All I can suggest is you make him as comfortable as possible."

Brendan said nothing. He merely nodded in acknowledgment of the doctor's words of advice.

And then, as Shelby watched, he moved away from her and crossed to his father's door.

Chapter Ten

Shelby wanted to go into his father's room with Brendan. She wanted to do something, to play mediator, nurse, referee or anyone else who might be necessary in order to mend the pain. She wanted to somehow smooth out the horrible awkwardness that existed between father and son. The diagnosis was bad enough to hear concerning a loved one. Added to the painful situation that Brendan found himself in, it was almost intolerable.

She wanted to help.

But she stayed where she was, knowing that they needed time alone. Knowing that Brendan had to make his own peace with it all.

After a moment she realized that the doctor was still standing in the hall next to her, quietly looking at her. She roused herself. "When will you be discharging him?" she asked.

"Are you a family friend, Shelby?" The doctor's voice was kind.

"Yes." Shelby looked toward the closed door, wishing she could see beyond it. "I am."

"Well, I don't think there's too much more that can be accomplished by keeping Mr. Connery here. We'll observe him for a few more days, but after that he can go home. I'll leave his prescriptions at the desk, or with you, Shelby, if you'd prefer."

"That'll be fine." She nodded, only half hearing him. A few more days. She was going to have to move fast. The hospital was not going to be happy about this. But it wasn't their happiness she was concerned about.

"He'll need phenytoin to control any possible seizure that might occur. And codeine pills to counteract the pain if there is any. There might not be," he told her hopefully. "He might be lucky."

Lucky. It was an odd word to apply to a man who was dying. Poor Danny, she thought, her heart aching. But most of all, poor Brendan.

Shelby stood outside the door and waited.

Brendan had only taken one step inside the room after he had closed the door. He stood, silent, his sophisticated manner stripped, useless. In desperation he searched for his anger, his constant, ready shield. But it was hard to be angry with Danny Connery when he looked so worn, so beaten lying there in bed. That pathetic old man, that shrunken shell, was his father. His *father.*

No!

He pushed the thought away. That poor excuse for a human being *wasn't* his father. His father was the dark-haired, vibrant man with laughing eyes whom he had locked away in his memory, if not his heart. The man before him was someone Brendan didn't know.

But someone who evoked pity from him, no matter how much he tried to deny it.

"Danny?" Danny Connery asked uncertainly, afraid of the dark look he saw on his son's face.

"Not Danny," Brendan corrected. "It's Brendan."

"Sorry." The apology came quickly. Danny tried to sit up, but it was obvious that he was still too weak and groggy to prop himself up. He needed help.

Brendan came forward reluctantly. But at least there was something to talk about for a moment, a distraction. "Do you want to sit up?"

The round head bobbed twice. Danny was grateful for the attention. "If you don't mind."

If you don't mind, Brendan thought, repeating the words in his head. Polite words. Stilted words. *I minded you leaving. Did you ever think of asking me that? Did you ask me then?*

Refraining from spitting out the accusation, Brendan silently pressed the control on the guard railing that raised the head of the bed. It made a slight whining noise as it lifted. Danny's face rose before him until they were almost eye-to-eye.

"Better?" Brendan asked.

"Fine." Danny flashed a smile. There was a tooth missing on one side. Brendan remembered that his father's smile had always seemed so bright, so quick to light up a room. He chided himself. Those were only childish memories.

"So," Brendan asked, hating the situation he found himself in, hating the charade, "how are you, feeling?"

"Fuzzy." Danny cleared his throat. "I could use a—" His father broke off sheepishly. His lips moved spasmodically in a rueful smile. "Old habits are hard to break."

And old wounds are hard to forget, Brendan countered silently.

"The doctor said that you're going to have to break them. No smoking, no drinking." Brendan laid the edict down firmly. He wished that there was space to move in the little room. He couldn't pace. There was nowhere to go but where he was.

Danny shrugged. The pale-blue-and-white hospital gown slipped a little on one shoulder. "What good'll that do me now?"

Did he suspect? No, he was just being dramatic. It was the one thing he had always been good at, Brendan thought. "Aren't you the one who used to dream?" Brendan couldn't keep the edge of sarcasm out of his voice. "The one who used to say that anything was possible?"

The words were an accusation and Danny didn't miss it. He sighed, shrinking even farther into his pillow. "I was a fraud."

"Yes, you were." The hurt, the disappointment, the anger were all there.

Danny turned away from his son, unable to face the consequences of his actions. Now, as then, he had no courage.

Silence hung heavily in the small room. Brendan wanted desperately to leave, to hurry away as quickly as possible, leaving all this behind him.

He knew that he couldn't. Slowly, he began again. "You don't have a place to stay, do you?"

He didn't want pity. Not from his own son. "I'll manage," Danny said quickly. There was a touch of the old pride in his statement. Danny licked his lips. They felt cracked, dry. "I wanted to thank you for paying for all this." Weakly he gestured about the room. "The nurse told me. Shelby."

Yes, he should have realized that Shelby would tell him, Brendan thought.

Danny stared at the clear-liquid bottle tethered to the IV in his arm. "I don't deserve it after what I've done to you."

"You won't get an argument from me about that part." Brendan shoved his hands into his trouser pockets. Unable to leave, unable to pace, he did the only thing that was left to him. He moved to the window.

The wind was up tonight and the sailboats were tilting into it as they turned for shore and home. Home. He hadn't really had one in all these years. Just a place where he ate and slept. A place with furnishings that were tasteful and expensive and met with the approval of his senior partners when they came to dinner with their wives. But it wasn't home. The last place that had been home to him was a tiny apartment where there had been someone to love him, to care if he lived or died.

There hadn't been anyone to care in a long time, not since his mother had died. In his own way, fearing the ultimate pain of rejection, he had seen to that.

Brendan made up his mind. He turned around to look at Danny. "You're coming back with me."

Danny was completely surprised by Brendan's offer. "You're taking me in?"

"Yes."

Danny's face broke into a toothy grin of joy. "Oh, Dan—Brendan, I don't know what to say." Tears welled up in place of words.

"That'll be a first." Brendan laughed shortly, not wanting any memories to warm him. They came anyway. "You could always talk."

Danny tried to reach for Brendan's hand, his fingers just barely making contact. Stiffly, Brendan moved away. He would take him in, pay for his bills, have his needs taken care of. That was his responsibility and he would face it.

But he wasn't going to open himself up to this man again, or to anyone. He refused. He couldn't take the jagged disappointment that would follow in its wake if he did.

Danny dropped his hand back on the bed. A little bit at a time. Perhaps, in time, he'd find a way. "I've got a confession to make, Brendan."

Brendan turned away, not wanting to hear whatever it was that Danny wanted to say. He didn't want the things that Danny stirred within him to rise. Compassion, pity, these were all emotions he didn't want to feel for the man. Yet they were there, nettling him, coming to life.

"If you have a confession to make, I'll get you a priest."

"No, not that kind of a confession, Danny-boy. It's just that, all these years, I didn't care about living or dying. It was all one and the same to me. And somehow, I just kept on living. Isn't that funny? I kept on living."

Where were the words to make his son understand? How could he make Brendan understand when he didn't? "But now, now that I see you, now that I'm here." His eyes moved slowly around the room. "I'm afraid of it. Dying." His voice lowered, hoarse for the fear in it. "I'm not ready anymore."

He turned and looked at Brendan in supplication, as if he could make it be different. "I don't want to die, Danny."

Very heavily, Brendan laid a hand on the gnarled one clutching at the blanket. "You're not going to die, old man." He couldn't bring himself to call him "Father." It just wouldn't come. "You're too tough and too ornery to die." Brendan had no idea where the lie came from. He only knew that the old man needed it. And so he had said it.

"Yeah, maybe you're right."

Danny rolled Brendan's words around in his mind. They had been sharp and short, but he clung to them like a drowning man to a plank of wood, taking solace, hoping it would preserve him. If Brendan said it was so, it was so. The doctors with their solemn expressions and their long white coats had frightened him, and the pains in his head, the demons that rose up in the night, they were only that. Demons of drink. Nothing more. He wasn't going to die. His son had promised it.

Danny asked no more questions, wanting to get no closer to the truth of his condition than he was at this moment.

Brendan considered telling him. Lies didn't sit well with him and telling the old man the truth would have given him the revenge he had so dearly wanted all those years ago when his adolescence had been snatched away. But somehow he couldn't do it. He just couldn't tell him. When he thought he would, blue eyes materialized in his mind, holding him back, stilling his tongue. It wasn't in him to cause hurt. That was something she had told him. Something she seemed to know that he didn't.

But he couldn't say it.

Brendan cleared his throat, uncomfortable with the look in Danny's eyes. "I've got to go."

"Yes, yes, a busy man you are. She told me. Shelly. She told me how important you are."

Brendan didn't need to be told who "she" was, or even why she had said what she had. He could see the effects of her words. Danny's eyes shone with pride when he looked at his son, the boy who had become everything his father could not. She had given an old man something to be proud of.

"She talks too much," Brendan murmured.

"No, never too much. I like her." Danny shifted in the bed, favoring his sore arm with its IV. "And I read about you myself. It was in a newspaper I used to cover myself, how you helped that man who was accused unfairly. You're a fine barrister, Danny."

The image his words generated brought a shiver up Brendan's spine. Covering himself with a newspaper. The man was a homeless transient. God, what had Danny Connery let himself become?

No, it was no concern of his. He was through caring. He'd do what he had to do, but he wouldn't care. He couldn't.

Brendan lowered the bed again, avoiding his father's eyes. "Get some sleep." He turned his back and moved to the door.

"Will you come back?' Danny called after his son anxiously.

"I'll come back," Brendan answered without turning around.

Danny sighed and the tension that riddled his body eased away.

Brendan stepped out of the room, closing the door behind him. Without thinking, he leaned his forehead against the door, his eyes closed. He felt so incredibly drained.

"Are you all right?"

Her voice startled him. He might have known she'd be waiting. Brendan straightened and nodded as he turned toward her.

He looked so pale, so drawn, she thought, wanting to reach out and stroke his face. "Did you tell him what he has?"

Slowly he shook his head. "I couldn't."

Thank God, she thought. She didn't think that Danny was a man who could handle something like this. There was no strength within him, no hope to draw on. Knowing would only make his last days unbearable. It was best to keep this from him as long as possible.

Shelby touched Brendan's shoulder lightly, making him look at her. "You're a good person, Brendan Connery."

For once, he was not warmed by the wattage in her smile. "Yeah, a regular Eagle Scout."

Brendan looked over his shoulder toward the door. This wasn't going to be good, he thought, not for any of them. But there was no turning back.

"This is your home?" Danny asked, peering out of the back-seat window of Brendan's silver Mercedes sedan. The words were swaddled in hushed awe. Ever since the conversation with Brendan three nights ago, Danny had looked forward to this moment, looked forward to being brought to his son's house. The trip from the hospital, though short, had tired him. But he had come to life at the sight of the imposing house.

Brendan glanced at Shelby in the front seat. He opened the door on the driver's side and got out. "This is where I live."

His choice of words went unnoticed by his father, but Shelby picked it up immediately. It wasn't his home. It was just a place he lived. Where was home for him, she wondered.

Shelby got out quickly and came around to the back. Brendan had already taken the rented wheelchair out of the trunk. Propping it open he stood contemplating the footrest in his hand.

He looked at Shelby impatiently. "How do you hook this damn thing up?"

"Easy," she said sweetly, knowing that he probably wanted to wring her neck. "Here." She took the footrest from him. "Let me do it."

Bending down, she secured the footrest through the two hinges on the wheelchair. "Second footrest." She held up her hand expectantly. Brendan gave it to her, muttering something unintelligible under his breath. Shelby secured the second footrest in identical fashion, snapping it into place.

"There." She winked as she stood up. "Magic." She brushed off her hands.

"Don't get sarcastic." Brendan got behind the wheelchair and pushed it to Danny's side of the car. "I would have gotten it sooner or later."

"I have no doubts," she answered. The amusement in her eyes told him differently.

She went to help Danny out of the car. The older man was still staring at the house, plainly mesmerized. He craned his neck to look at his son. "It's grand, Danny-boy."

Shelby saw the frown that rose up in response to the name. "'Danny?'" she repeated. Brendan's frown deepened. "Is that your real name?" she asked him.

"It was." Brendan's tone allowed no further exploration of the topic.

She didn't need to. It was easy to see that Brendan had wanted to divest himself of all memory of his father. For that matter, she was surprised that he hadn't changed his surname, as well.

She turned her mind to her duties. This afternoon had been a hectic one. There had been a hasty party in her honor, thrown by the nurses on the floor. Several others had popped by to say goodbye and wish her well. Harris Memorial and three years of dedication were now behind her. She was in Brendan's employ.

"Here," she prompted the old man, "let me have your hands." She wrapped her fingers firmly around the fragile wrists and gently pulled him forward until he stood wavering, on his feet. "See, you can do it. Slowly, slowly," she urged, turning his body so that he could sit in the wheelchair.

Awkwardly, releasing a gratified sigh, Danny made it into the chair and sat down.

"And we have contact," Shelby said, taking care to sound cheerful. "Okay, I'll take it from here." She moved Brendan out of the way and took ahold of the wheelchair.

Brendan was more than happy to let her take over. He closed the doors on his car and then went to unlock the front door of his house. Placing his key in the ornamental lock, he punched a series of numbers on the rectangular pad next to the door frame, disconnecting the security system.

Danny took it all in with wide eyes, as if he were on the verge of entering a world that he had only imagined in dreams.

"You live well, boy."

Brendan only looked at him, his brow raised, wondering if the old man had the slightest inkling of the way he really lived because of him. Wondering if the old man knew that he had prohibited him from ever living well.

She wasn't exactly sure what was going on between the two; she only knew it wasn't good for her patient. Or for the man she was growing to care for very much. "It's very nice," Shelby said, breaking the silence. "Shall we go in now, Brendan?"

Brendan held the door open, letting them pass through first.

The tile in the entranceway was a light champagne beige. There was a staircase in the center, with cream rugs, leading up to the second floor. A chandelier hung over it, illuminating the foyer that fanned out in either direction. On one side it led to a huge living room with a conversation pit surrounding the fireplace. The other side fed into a country-sized kitchen that looked as if it had been decorated by someone bent on creating a gourmet's workplace. There was a great deal of work space, with brightly polished copper pots hanging overhead. Beyond that was a bedroom with a separate bath. His father's room.

For now, Brendan thought stoically.

Shelby was certain she had never seen any place that looked quite as beautiful. Or quite as cold. The colors were not warm. They brought icy images to mind. She shifted her eyes to Brendan. The man definitely did not.

There was discord here, discord she promised herself to get to the bottom of and resolve. Everyone deserved happiness.

But for now, the basic chores had to be attended to. "I think we should get him to his room," she told Brendan, nodding at Danny. "He's probably very tired."

Danny turned slightly in his chair to nod his agreement. "That I am, Shelly."

Though he looked tired, it was obvious that his spirits had brightened. Shelby knew that it had been the right move for the old man. She only prayed that it was for Brendan.

"It's in the back of the house," Brendan said, leading the way.

The guest room was decorated in the same colors as the rest of the house. Beiges and browns. A large double bed with a brown velvet cover was the center of the room. There was a nightstand on either side. A mournful painting of the last days of autumn, with trees denuded of their leaves, took up most of one wall.

Danny looked at his son uncertainly, as if unable to believe that this was really true. Two weeks ago, before he had walked into the mission, he had slept in a cardboard box beneath an overpass. Now he was in his son's house, a son he had lost track of until recently. "And I'm to stay here?"

Brendan misunderstood the tone of disbelief in the man's voice. "You don't like it?"

"Oh, it's wonderful, just wonderful," Danny said quickly, afraid of giving offense. "But I don't want to put you out of your room."

Brendan stood in the doorway, as if unable to come farther into the room his father was to occupy. "You're not. I sleep upstairs."

Danny remembered the tiny apartment he had last shared with his son and wife. The flophouses that had come afterward. "More bedrooms?"

"Three."

Danny shook his head in wonder. "Such a big house for only one man."

Brendan shrugged, his arms folded before him. "I like getting the most for my money."

Danny forgot himself and momentarily played the role of father. He was rusty at it. "You should have a family, boy."

"Yes." Brendan looked pointedly at his father. "I should. But it didn't work out that way, did it?" He didn't wait for an answer. It was evident in the chagrined expression on the man's face. "Can I get you anything?"

Danny shook his head. "No, maybe later."

"Later," Brendan agreed.

He looked uncomfortable, Shelby thought. How long was it going to take to eradicate that? How much time did they have?

"Do you want any help?" Brendan asked, but didn't move from where he was.

Danny took the inquiry to be directed to him. "No, Shelly and I'll manage."

Brendan looked at Shelby, a question in his eyes.

"I'll just be a few minutes," she assured him. "Relax. I know what I'm doing. It's what you're paying me for, isn't it?"

"Yes, I suppose it is." Brendan left the room. She watched him go. The tension he felt was evident in his shoulders.

Oh, God, Shelby thought, had she done the right thing by pushing this? She fervently hoped so.

Chapter Eleven

Shelby slipped quietly out of Danny's room. Though the old man had been slightly keyed up over his new surroundings, she was satisfied that he would have a good night.

She found Brendan in the living room. He was standing at the window, gazing out at nothing. One look at his shoulders told her that his tension hadn't diminished.

He watched her walk toward him in the reflection in the window, moving like something out of a man's dream, though not one of his. He didn't have dreams like that. He seldom dreamed at all. If he did, when he woke he never remembered what it was that he had dreamed about. Only that it left behind a feeling of emptiness, of bereavement and loss.

Brendan watched as she raised a hand to touch his shoulder. She moved with assurance, with confidence.

He wondered if she ever harbored any doubts. Probably not. She seemed oblivious to things like that.

He turned to face her. "I think he'll probably sleep through the night," Shelby told him.

She saw the doubts in his eyes, the uncertainty. His expression was calm and gave away nothing that he was thinking. But his eyes did.

"That's good." He loosened his tie.

She hadn't realized until then that he was still wearing his suit. He hadn't made himself comfortable while she'd been putting his father to bed.

Because he wasn't comfortable, she thought.

"I'll be here in the morning. At eight." She watched his face, wishing that she could say something to him to ease the disquiet. She hadn't meant to cause him any hardship. "Will you be all right with this?" she asked softly.

An ironic half smile played on his lips. "A little late to wonder, isn't it?" She began to answer, but he shook his head. "No, I'll be fine. Fine."

The repeated word trailed away from him and faded into the air, nonexistent. He wasn't going to be fine at all, and he knew it, not while he and his father were under the same roof.

Her heart ached for him. He needed to reconcile himself with so many things. With himself, with his father. With his own feelings and the fact that he still had them, no matter what he thought to the contrary.

She touched his arm gently. "Would you like me to stay the night?"

He started, caught completely off guard by the suggestion. "What?" As her question replayed itself in his head, he knew he wanted nothing more than to have her spend the night.

"Would you like me to stay the night?" she repeated. "In case your father needs something. It might make you rest easier." *And make everyone feel better all around,* she added silently.

When she had asked, he hadn't been thinking of her as a nurse. He found he had trouble thinking of her as anything but a woman.

Brendan glanced off in the direction of his father's room. It might take the edge off his agitation. having her here to take care of Danny if anything should occur. He had no idea what to expect.

"Yes, I suppose it might." He looked down at her face.

And then again, maybe it wouldn't, he thought, feeling responses vibrate through him, begging to be set free. He was an adult, he told himself firmly. He didn't give in to demands unless he wanted to. He was in control. "Would you mind?"

She shook her head. "I'm a nurse. I'm used to putting in strange hours on short notice." She watched as Brendan pulled off his tie altogether, and them removed his jacket, draping them on the back of the sofa. "Besides, I'm more or less on my own in this, so I can decide whether or not I should stretch my hours."

She began making a mental list of things she would need to pick up in order to spend the night. It would take her forty-five minutes to go home and return. "All I have to do is put in a call to Irene and she can reschedule the other nurse."

He had thought that she was going to be here all the time. He'd given no thoughts to there being anyone else on the premises. "Other nurse?"

She wondered if he knew that he was cute when he was bewildered. She doubted anyone had the courage to tell him that.

"Uh-huh. We'll work in shifts. Two six-hour shifts should do it, I think, unless you want three." Brendan was frowning now. "What's the matter?"

"Nothing." He shook his head, but she could see that there was clearly something wrong. "I just thought that you'd be here when I came home at night...."

It was hard enough accepting having his father here. Accepting two strangers was even more difficult for him. He didn't think to question the fact that having Shelby here wasn't hard at all.

Shelby considered his objection. "I could take the afternoon shift."

"And when I left for work in the morning."

She tilted her head back, laughter in her eyes. "Slavery went out over a hundred years ago," she said, amused. "Or haven't you heard?"

Brendan didn't explore the reasons for his feelings. He went for the obvious explanation. "It's just that he's used to you." He nodded in the direction of his father's room. "And I'm used to you." The words had just slipped out. He hadn't meant them to.

"Are you?" Shelby cocked one brow, studying him. *Are you, now,* she wondered.

He had had more sophistication at his disposal when he had presented his very first case in court. Why was he fumbling now? Because this was too important to him. He became annoyed with himself.

"It would make things easier, that's all." He picked up his jacket from the sofa and walked toward the stairs. "Never mind—"

"Brendan," Shelby called after him.

He stopped and turned only slightly, as if he had conceded too much already. "What?"

Shelby smiled at him. It was a confident smile, an encouraging one. It amazed him how much could be packed into something seemingly so insignificant and small. "It's going to be all right."

"Is it?" He had never been an optimist. And there was so much that was wrong here, so much he didn't know how to deal with.

"Yes." She remained where she was by the sofa, her fingers laced together. Never had he seen anyone look more confident. Or more appealing. "Somehow, it is."

Brendan crossed back into the room and shrugged. It hadn't been all right in so many years. Why should it be any different now? With so much going against this situation involving his father and him, why should things be better? "If you say so."

Shelby took Brendan's hand and led him to the conversation pit. "I say so. C'mon, why don't you sit down and unwind? You're so tense you're going to snap."

"I am not tense," he told her as she sat him down on the top step of the conversation pit. They could have sat on the sofa, but somehow the conversation pit seemed more appropriate.

Shelby moved behind him and began kneading his neck muscles. "Yes, you are. I've seen less rigid mountain ranges."

"You don't have to do that." But even as he said it, something within him almost sighed for the relief that he felt.

"You might as well reap some of the benefits of having a nurse around. I give a very mean back rub. My family loves me for my hands."

She laughed softly and he absorbed the sound. For a moment he allowed himself to enjoy the sensations that throbbed through his body, sensations diametrically opposed to each other. She was relieving one tension and fueling another.

Shelby could feel the tenseness leave his shoulders and neck. At least this much she could do for him, she thought. She glanced around at the conversation pit as she continued massaging. "I've only seen these in model houses. Do you really use it?"

He had no idea what she was talking about. "What? The fireplace?"

"No, the conversation pit." She sat back on her heels, but continued kneading the knot in his neck. "Do you sit here by the fire and talk and look into the flames for answers?"

She was an incredible romantic. He wondered how she got to be her age and still retain that quality. "Answers aren't found in flames, Shelby." He turned to look at her. "There aren't any answers."

Shelby let her hands slowly drop to her sides. The pain in his eyes tore at her heart. "Yes, there are. The questions have to be worded correctly, that's all." Shelby sank back on the first step and kicked off her shoes, her toes sinking into the plush beige rug. It felt luxurious. And unused.

"This is lovely." She leaned back on her hands and looked into the fireplace. "Too bad there's no fire."

He laughed at the bald attempt to prompt him. "That's a hint, isn't it?"

She leaned her head back, her hair lightly skimming down her back. Her grin was impish. "You're very quick."

No, he thought, he wasn't nearly quick enough. If he was quick, he could have outrun Shelby, outrun the sensations she created in him before they had taken hold so tenaciously.

He could still break free, he told himself, rising to get some kindling from the basket next to the fireplace. It was just a matter of effort, that was all.

And that was the problem, he thought as he tossed the kindling into the fireplace. He couldn't summon the effort to do it. But he would. In time.

Keeping his mind strictly on his task, he took one of the long matches he kept next to the basket and struck it, then tossed it into the kindling. The flames started almost instantly. He moved the grating back into place. Glancing at her, he saw that Shelby was staring into the flames. What did *she* see there that he couldn't, he wondered.

"Satisfied?" Brendan asked as he dropped down next to her. He leaned his elbows on the step behind him and stretched out. It felt right. Having her here felt right. He knew it was all a delusion, but for now he would let it go on. He could always stop it when the time came.

"Very," she answered. Languidly she pulled her hands through her hair and then let it fall again.

It had been a warm day, but the temperature had dropped down by some fifteen degrees or so. The warmth from the fire was welcomed. The one from within was another matter. Brendan regarded Shelby's profile in silence for a moment, wondering what it was about her that attracted him so. It had been there from the very first, pulling at him, leading him to this moment.

Leading him to certain disaster.

She wasn't extraordinarily beautiful. Her nose was a bit too pointy, her mouth too wide and her eyes were just the slightest bit too far apart. If he had been painting, he would have improved the pieces. But the sum. He could never have improved on the sum. Something happened when they all came together. The whole was greater than the sum of its parts. A gregarious, compelling woman emerged when they were put together, a woman who preyed on his mind long after she disappeared from view.

Brendan wondered what he was going to do about all this. And if it was already too late to try.

Shelby leaned back and sighed, her hair brushing along the step behind her. The sigh that escaped was one of contentment. "This feels wonderful. I've been running around all day." She turned to look at him, a bittersweet expression playing on her face. "Leaving a place is never easy."

He resisted the urge to play with the ends of her hair. Touching would lead to trouble. "If you didn't want to leave the hospital, Shelby, why did you?"

"Irene was right." She saw that the name meant nothing to him. "My sister, remember?" He nodded, but she could tell that he didn't. There were other things on his mind. "She said it was time for me to move on. And it was. Besides, I couldn't disappoint your father."

She saw the slight darkening in his eyes. It had been the wrong thing to say. But it was the truth. At least partially. And she could not function if she had to measure every word constantly.

His stiffness had returned. "No, we couldn't have that, could we?"

She couldn't bear to see him go on this way. "Let it go, Brendan."

He didn't understand. "Let what go?"

"The anger." He tried to turn from her, but she wouldn't let him. The touch of her hand kept him in place. "The hurt. It's eating at you."

Brendan shook his head slowly. "There's nothing left inside for it to eat. He saw to that."

But it wasn't that easy. She wasn't going to let him hide behind an excuse. "No, you did. You could have put it aside."

"I did. I locked it all away."

She touched his cheek. "No, not all."

He couldn't stay angry when she touched him. He couldn't even stay firm in his resolve. "Being a Peeping Tom again?"

"Yes." Her smile lit the corners of her eyes, making his stomach turn over.

Flip-flops. Adolescent feelings. No, not quite adolescent. Adolescence anticipated but did not know. He knew, or thought he knew, what there was ahead.

He knew his limits. And he had reached them. Her nearness was affecting him, crowding in under his skin, stirring him, pushing everything else aside. By all rights, either his own personal turmoil or the murder trial he was gathering information about should have totally occupied his time, his mind, his last drop of energy. At the very least, trials always did.

And yet, this woman with her extra-wide smile was forcing everything else into the background every time she came close to him. The only things that moved to the fore were his feelings.

No, he didn't have feelings. He had stripped himself of that years ago. Feelings were for fools.

And he, Brendan thought, had just taken on the role of jester.

He looked lost in thought, though his eyes were on her. "So you want me to stay?" Shelby asked softly.

"Yes." Gently, unable to stop himself, he framed her face between his hands. "I want you to stay."

Her pulse quickened as desires slammed through her body. She found it difficult to swallow. "I'll just go home and get some things."

His eyes were on hers. "No," he said softly. But it bound her to him.

The words in her mind tumbled over one another in confusion. "I need something to sleep in."

He was touching her face lightly, gently, as if his fingertips were kissing her. As if they were already making love to her. "Not tonight," he whispered.

She saw the desire rise in his eyes. "All right." She wasn't certain if she had said the words aloud or not, her heart was hammering so loud.

She watched him, her eyes huge, as he drew her closer to him. He could see his own reflection in her eyes. He was trapped there, he thought. She held him trapped within her. He had always been, first and foremost, a survivor. The terms of his life had dictated that. And he knew that to lose himself in her would not be just a momentary finding of pleasure. This would be different. Once done, he would be irrevocably lost. His world would unravel. *He* would unravel.

He knew all that, knew the consequences. Feared the consequences so that his breath caught in his throat. But he couldn't let go. Not of her, not of the ever-increasing hum of expectation, of desire that was zipping through his entire body in a jagged pattern.

Damn!

He damned himself for needing and damned her for being sweet and giving, for being there when he was so vulnerable. For one taste of heaven, he knew in his heart he was going to put himself through everlasting hell.

It should have been enough to stop him. It didn't even begin. To need, to love, meant to be hurt, and he had been hurt enough for one lifetime. If he was to flee, it would be now.

He stopped playing the devil's advocate. He stopped playing.

His mouth lowered to hers and she almost moaned from the desire gripping her in its viselike hold. It was the gasp of a rider as the roller coaster came to a halt, tottering on the brink of the highest peak, poised for a plunging descent. Shelby grabbed and hung on for dear life.

This time Brendan didn't even try to be gentle. If he frightened her, if he made her withdraw, then maybe it would be better for both of them. Maybe there was time to stop what was happening before it was too late. But she had to be the one to stop it. He hadn't the strength anymore.

And even that scared the hell out of him. He had never been so afraid of anything in his life, not even of being alone. But he was frightened now, frightened of having his soul ripped out of him and placed in the hands of this woman with laughing eyes, this woman who spoke of inherent goodness in everyone.

This woman who would hurt him.

Her back was against the steps and they were digging in. She hardly felt the imprint. Far greater was the imprint of his lips on hers, the burning press of his hard body, hot and demanding, on hers. Her arms encircled his neck, pulling him closer as she met his passions one for one and gave him more.

She arched her body, seeking his warmth, wanting desperately to be touched. She wanted to feel his hands on her, possessing each part he stroked. She tried to tell him, but words turned into sounds, into moans, and died away as he kissed her mouth over and over again.

Though he wasn't gentle, he made her feel desirable, special. Beautiful. She had never felt this starved intensity before, laced with awe, with worship. It wasn't just a pleasant experience. It was the *only* experience.

Shelby shuddered as his hands left her hair and roamed over her body, claiming, exploring, caressing. She had wanted nothing more than to soothe him. He was troubled and he needed her, needed her help. But now she was helpless to do anything except respond to the sensations that were pounding through her. Sensations she had never felt before.

As his mouth crushed against hers, she groaned, trying to pull him closer, through her, in her.

If he didn't catch his breath, he was going to be swept away into the eye of a whirlwind. "Am I hurting you?" he asked after a beat, waiting until he thought his voice was steady. It wasn't.

"You're not," she answered, her lips reddened from the pressure of his mouth, "but the steps are."

"Shelby." Her name hung in the air. Brendan tried to pull himself together and couldn't. He wanted her, now, but at what price? "I—"

She made it easy for him. For them. "Take me to your room."

He rose and swept her up in his arms. She had him wanting to laugh even as his freedom was slipping away. The power she had over him was frightening. "Is the other nurse this demanding?"

She pretended to think, linking her arms around his neck. "I've just rescheduled nurses. You'll be getting Rhonda."

"Rhonda? Sexy name," he teased as he crossed to the staircase.

"Rhonda got her nursing certificate in the marines. She's six-one and strictly a no-nonsense type. She's also a grandmother four times over and has an insanely jealous husband."

"I take it you don't care for competition?"

"Nope." Shelby buried her face in his neck, her body taut like a bow. "Not where it matters."

Brendan told himself that it was her warm breath on his neck that made him shiver. But in his heart he knew that it was her words that did it.

He pushed open the door to his room with his shoulder. It was dark inside, but he didn't bother reaching for the light. There was moonlight streaming in through the parted curtains to cast aside the darkness. It was all they needed.

Brendan sat Shelby down beside his bed. He could hear nothing but the sound of their breathing, as charged expectations seared the air. Shelby stood very, very still as Brendan slowly undid the buttons on her blouse. He felt her quiver beneath his fingers. Painstakingly he slipped the blouse from her shoulders, savoring every second, every inch of skin that was exposed to him. She was wearing ice blue satin beneath the blouse. He could make out the tempting curve of her breasts.

Brendan hooked one finger beneath an ice blue strap. "What is that?"

"A teddy."

He let the strap sag off her shoulder. "Women really wear things like that?"

"Seems so."

Shelby sucked in her breath as he opened the button on her skirt. While his lips teased hers, she felt his hands lifting the skirt higher and higher on her legs, gently probing as he reached her thighs. She thought her knees would buckle and she held on to his shoulders for support.

Pressing her to him, searing her with the hot imprint of his wanting body, he pulled down the zipper on her hip and her skirt dropped to the floor.

"It's very pretty," he whispered against her skin. "The teddy," he added when he saw the question in her eyes. "I don't want to rip it. Take it off for me."

Though her body burned, Shelby stepped back and slipped her fingers beneath the strap on her shoulder, letting it slide down, her eyes on him. His face was partially hidden in shadows. But the look in his eyes, the flame of desire, was enough to mesmerize her.

The teddy sagged, catching on the swollen peaks of Shelby's breasts. Brendan reached out and tugged ever so slightly, fighting the desire to rip the flimsy fabric away from her.

Shelby caught her breath as the teddy sank to her waist.

"I think I can take it from here." Moving closer, Brendan placed his hands on either side of the swell of her hips. And then slowly, inch by inch, he slid his hands down her silken skin, until the teddy softly parachuted down to join the skirt, forgotten.

"Shouldn't you be taking something off?" Shelby asked. Her throat felt so tight the words had to be forced out of her mouth.

Brendan stripped off everything but his briefs.

"More..." she prompted in a seductive whisper, hooking her fingertips along the elastic waistband of his briefs. The heat they felt singed both of them before she was through, and they fell onto the bed, restraint gone, words fading.

There was nothing but the magic left.

Over and over again he kissed her, branding her face, the hollow of her throat, the valley between her breasts. Impatiently Shelby grasped his shoulders, dragging his mouth back up to hers. She wanted to give as well as receive, she wanted to make love as well as be made love to.

She wanted more than anything else in the world to share herself with him.

The generosity of her gifts overwhelmed him and broke down the last of his barriers. He crushed his mouth to hers as his hands moved in mounting circles, caressing her, possessing her. He thought he had control, he thought that he could restrain himself as long as he wanted.

He was wrong.

There was no control left. Only desire, painted white hot and vibrant. Unable to hold back the tide of emotions any longer, Brendan raised himself over Shelby and entered her. Always before when he had made love, it had been in rooms that were well lit. But he never remembered seeing a single face, a single expression at the final moment. Here, with just the moonlight to illuminate the room, he saw only her face. And in her face he saw everything in one blinding flash.

Brendan gasped out her name as he fell into paradise against his will.

Chapter Twelve

When Shelby woke the next morning it took her a moment to pull her thoughts together before she remembered where she was. In Brendan's bed. Alone. Without Brendan.

Bits and pieces came back to her in warm waves. First the recollection of last night, the passion, the tenderness that was shared. And then the loneliness of the room. Shelby's fingers spread out over his side of the bed. The sheets were cold. Brendan had gotten up and left her some time ago.

Why hadn't he wakened her? Why had he left her alone like this?

She sat up, pulling the sheet around her as best she could. A sliver of hope refused to be splintered with the rest. She looked toward the bathroom. "Brendan?"

But there was no response. There wasn't a sound to be heard. Everything was still, quiet. Lonely.

Shelby ran her hands through her hair. Her emotions were running rampant. Exhilaration and depression were blending, mixing together. He had been so loving last night. So powerful, yet so tender. How could he not be here now? She gave her heart easily, caring for people. But her body was something else entirely. That she only shared when she loved.

A small sigh escaped. She felt as if she had been slapped and her first reaction was to feel a self-preserving anger flashing through her.

How dare he? How dare he just use her like this and then go? Didn't he realize that this wasn't the end? That this was just the beginning for them?

Maybe he didn't. Shelby sighed again and ran her hands up and down her arms. Maybe Brendan didn't want beginnings, only endings. She told herself to forget about him. To do the job she was hired to do, do what she had a calling for, and leave Brendan Connery to his own demons.

Easier said than done. She gave great pep talks. But she was her own worst audience. She'd go on caring and go on trying. Shelby knew she might as well resign herself to that.

With the sheet tucked around her like a long, trailing sarong, Shelby rose from the bed. As she did, a piece of paper fluttered to the carpet next to her foot. She stooped to pick it up, struggling to keep the sheet in place.

The note was from Brendan. "Had to leave early. Sorry."

"I bet you are," she murmured to herself, looking at the five sterile words. "But you've bitten off more than you can chew this time. Afraid of intimacy, are you,

Brendan Connery?'' Shelby tossed her hair back carelessly. "We'll just have to get you over that."

She only hoped she could.

Throwing the end of the sheet over her shoulder,
Shelby crossed to the bathroom. She had no time to let
herself sink into pity, even if she was so inclined. There
was a patient waiting for her.

He let himself in quietly that evening, wondering what
he was going to say to her. There was no excuse for
leaving her alone this morning. Certainly not the one he
had so hastily written down on the piece of paper. It
hadn't been work that had made him flee so early. It had
been fear, fear of the future, fear of his own feelings.
Fear of her. After they had made love, he had lain awake
most of the night, thinking. Anticipating an end. Life
hadn't prepared him to believe in anything else.

He remembered that he had told her he never ran from
anything. It was an odd feeling to realize that he was a
liar.

"Shelby?" His own voice echoed back to him. Had
something gone wrong? Suddenly he forgot about the
feelings that had caused him to leave so early, and
crossed to the living room, genuine concern overcom-
ing everything else. "Shelby?"

"She's not here, Mr. Connery. Her shift ended at
noon."

Brendan turned to see that the soft-spoken voice belonged to a pleasant-looking, heavyset, tall woman with
gray hair, who was emerging from the kitchen. She was
wearing a nurse's tunic and pants, with an insignia on
her pocket neatly proclaiming Angels of Mercy.

He blinked, trying to make a connection. "And you
are?"

"Rhonda." She stepped forward and clasped his hand in hers, shaking it heartily.

The grandmother with the marine background, Brendan remembered. He tried his best to hide the disappointment he felt, mainly from himself. He couldn't afford to risk entanglements. He had sworn off them over twenty years ago. It had been his way of coping with the devastating hurt his young heart had endured. He hadn't been enough of a reason for his father to stay. He didn't matter enough for his mother to want to go on living. He couldn't ever go through caring and not mattering again.

So why did he wish that she was here?

Rhonda looked at the watch on her wide wrist. "It's after five. I'll be leaving myself within the hour. Your father's eaten and is resting comfortably."

Brendan barely remembered to mutter, "That's good," before he walked out of the foyer. He left the nurse looking after him curiously as he went up to his room.

He opened the double doors. For some wild, inexplicable reason, he realized that he actually half expected Shelby to still be here, where he had left her in the wee hours of the morning, her hair falling into her face, her soft breasts rising and falling as she slept. He had watched her for a long time last night.

She wasn't there.

She had made the bed. He stood in the doorway, picturing the way the room had been last night, bathed in moonlight and shadows. If he closed his eyes and tried, he could still catch the tiniest whiff of her perfume.

Brendan sat on the corner of the bed, wondering if he was coming unraveled.

Perfect timing, he upbraided himself. His client, a prominent politician, was up on charges of murder two. Brendan needed to be at his sharpest, not mired in some sort of an emotional muddle, fantasizing about a woman with red gold hair. The D.A. himself was trying this one, seeing it as some sort of a stepping stone for himself to bigger things.

Brendan laughed at the absurdity of it all. The D.A. was sharpening carving knives and his own mind was lost to him, of absolutely no use whatsoever because it was crowded with a panorama of scenes filled with her. And dark memories of the past.

The phone rang. There were a dozen different people who could be calling him for the same number of reasons. He knew it was Shelby.

He stretched back across the bed, securing the receiver, and lay down, cradling the phone against his neck. Wearily he folded his arms across his chest, daring fate to disappoint him. "Hello?"

Fate didn't disappoint him.

"You're finally home." Shelby's voice filtered through his head at the same instant that desire filtered through his body.

He wanted to tell her a hundred different things. That he was sorry. That last night had been something he had never experienced before and probably never would again. That he was firing her because she had no place upsetting his life like this. All the words tripped over one another, tangling in his mind. He said nothing.

What could he say? "Looks that way. I just met Rhonda."

She couldn't quite read the tone in his voice. Was he being distant? Annoyed? He had a hell of a nerve if it was that. She was the one who had been hurt, not him. "We never agreed to my hours."

His mind had always been precision sharp, and details were something he was good at. Except now. He couldn't recall the conversation, but bluffed his way through. "I thought we did."

She wondered if he was joking. "Twelve-hour shifts are a little long."

Brendan sat up, pulling his legs under him. He went with the impulse that seized him. "What if I paid you for your time?"

She didn't know what he was getting at. But she did notice a shift in his tone. It was more hopeful than it had been a moment ago. And more vulnerable. "You are."

"I mean more." He hesitated, then forged on. "To stay here."

She paused for a moment. Was he just asking for a full-time nurse, or was it something more? She held the telephone tightly in her hand. The eternal optimist, for once she was afraid to hope. "Are you serious?"

"Yes." And as he said it, he knew he was. "Shelby, I'd like to come home and see you here."

Such simple words, such a simple thought. Why was it so hard for him to ask? He didn't know. He only knew that it was the most difficult thing he had ever permitted himself to say.

"You have a funny way of showing it." All her anger disappeared. It always did in the face of pain, or embarrassment, or regret. She sensed all three.

"Shelby..." He paused, searching for the right words. "This is new to me."

She smiled to herself. *The big dummy.* "That makes two of us."

She didn't understand what he was saying, Brendan thought. "No, I don't think so."

Did he think that she slept around? The thought hurt and it showed in her voice. "Are we talking about the same thing? I don't do what I did last night easily."

"I don't do what I did last night at all." *I don't open up. I don't feel. I don't want to,* Brendan thought fiercely, as if that would erase it all.

What was he saying? "I'm sure you've been with plenty of women."

"Yes." There was no point in denying that. He hadn't been a monk. But neither had he ever been a lover in the true sense of the word.

She paused, waiting. But he added nothing more. What was he trying to tell her, she wondered. *You are a hell of a confusing man, Brendan Connery. Lucky for you I like puzzles.*

She glanced at her watch, quickly making plans. "Rhonda gets off at six." If she wanted to be there soon, she was going to have to hustle. "Do you want me to be a live-in nurse?"

I want you here, with me. I know I'm asking for trouble, but I don't seem to have a choice. "Yes." Brendan swung his legs over the side of the bed.

There was something more in his voice, something that helped her make up her mind. "I can be there in about an hour. You're going to make Irene very happy."

He knew he was signing his own death warrant. "That'll make one."

Shelby bit her lip. Try as she might not to let them, there were times his words hurt. "Sorry to hear that."

He heard her backing away. Damn. He didn't mean— "Shelby—"

"What?"

He tried again to apologize. And again he couldn't. "I'll see you in an hour."

Shelby replaced the receiver on her kitchen wall phone and stood looking at it for a moment. This was not going to be easy. But then, she had known as much when she had gotten involved. This wasn't coming as a surprise. What she hadn't realized was just how deeply she would be getting herself into all this.

But there were no regrets. Not yet, anyway.

Shelby went to pack.

It took her less than half an hour to pack and less than that to drive over. If a few misgivings nagged at her, she refused to examine them. She knew the chances she was taking, the risk that always came in getting involved. But somewhere along the line she had made up her mind that Brendan was worth it. She didn't know when. She just knew that she had.

Pulling into his driveway, Shelby parked her car and got out, suitcase in hand. She told herself that it was ridiculous to feel awkward. At the very least, she was here as a professional, a nurse. And at the most—well, they'd take that one step at a time and see.

She rang the bell and Brendan answered almost instantly, startling her. "It's a trick I learned from you," he said, noting the surprised look on her face. "You were standing behind the door when I came to pick you up, remember?"

Shelby walked in. "I just didn't want to go up the stairs again."

He took her suitcase from her and closed the door. "I thought you said you liked stairs."

"That's the trouble with lawyers, they remember too much." She took her sweater off and turned around. He was still standing with her suitcase, just looking at her. Probably having second thoughts, she decided.

"Shelby—"

"Brendan—"

They said each other's names simultaneously and then backed off at the same instant.

This was going to be up to her, she thought. If hurts were going to be healed, it was going to have to be up to her. At least in the beginning.

Brendan turned. "Your room is upstairs," he told her, leading the way.

She followed quickly, choosing her words as she went. "Brendan, I'm here as your father's nurse. Whatever else happens, happens." They came to the landing and she touched his arm, wanting him to look at her. She needed to see his eyes. "All right?"

Brendan drew a breath. The air needed clearing. "About last night . . ."

If he was going to apologize, to say that he hadn't meant last night to have happened, she was going to forget all about her good intentions, grab her suitcase from him and hit him with it.

"You don't owe me anything for last night," she said quickly. It was the first lie she had ever told him. He did owe her, she thought. He owed her the love she felt he was holding back. But she couldn't tell him that. Not yet. "But you owe yourself some honesty."

He placed the suitcase down in the doorway of the guest bedroom next to his. "What are you talking about?"

Shelby walked in, then turned to face him. "Nothing I can explain in a word or two."

"Or three."

"Or three," she agreed with a smile. "It's something that's going to have to be worked out."

Brendan nodded. For now, it was enough that she was here. Maybe she was right. Maybe the rest would work itself out somehow. "He's been asking for you."

She could settle in later, she thought, leaving her suitcase where it was. She headed for the stairs again. "How is he doing?"

Brendan caught up to her on the stairs and shrugged. "I don't know."

She stopped to look at him incredulously. "You don't know?"

He didn't like the tone she was using. "Rhonda said that—"

Shelby couldn't believe the thought that crossed her mind. "Haven't you been in to see him?"

"No." The word was both defensive and defiant.

Shelby backed off. "I see." She resumed walking down the stairs. The course of her conversation changed, lightened, but her mind was working at a furious pace.

There was a lot of work to be done here, she thought. A hell of a lot.

Shelby spent the next few days getting a routine under way. Her first priority was lifting Danny's spirits. Though the old man didn't talk about it, she surmised that he had his suspicions that he would never recover.

She cast about for things to get him involved in. She discovered, quite by accident, that he had once enjoyed playing poker.

"You just happen to be in luck," she informed him breezily. "I play a very mean hand myself."

"You?" Danny's eyes narrowed beneath his wispy brows. "You're a girl."

She laughed, amused. "And you're a chauvinist."

He shared the joke with her. He'd be anything she wanted him to be, though in his heart, women did have a definite place in the order of life. On pedestals. "Maybe I am."

"Well." She fluffed his pillow for him and tucked the cover in. "You're just going to have to put your money where your mouth is, Daniel Connery. I'm going to go out and get a deck of cards."

Danny loved it.

When she saw how much the old man was enjoying himself and how playing seemed to give Danny something to look forward to, Shelby talked her brother Tyler into coming over and joining them on his day off. Tyler brought Murphy.

"What are you doing here?" she asked the slighter, dark-haired man.

"My muse wouldn't come," he answered with a careless shrug.

Murphy was the family artist. When his muse was active, he constructed sheer poetry on canvas. Most of the time, though, he stood around waiting for something to speak to him.

"He says he's going through a blue period," Tyler confided.

"This'll help," Shelby promised her two older brothers, escorting them into the dining room, where Danny sat in his wheelchair, eager to play.

They played for hours. And it worked. Everyone's spirits rose, especially Danny's. Shelby did her best not to simply apply medication but to apply a healthy dose of life to an old man who had withdrawn from everything but the barest fringes of existence. As she watched Danny laugh and talk with her brothers, she knew she was succeeding far better with the senior Connery than she was with his son. Though she felt the electricity, felt the desire between them, Brendan hadn't come near her in nearly a week.

He arrived home late every evening and then closeted himself in his den, making notes on the upcoming trial until the wee hours of the morning. He didn't come to see his father, not at breakfast, not at dinner. Not at all. And he kept his contact with her at a minimum, as if he regretted his decision.

Shelby stood for it as long as she could.

Brendan looked up at the sound of the knock on his door. For a moment it startled him. He had forced himself into such a deep concentration that he had forgotten anyone else was in the house. He had lived alone for more years than he could remember. And old habits were hard to break. He recalled that that was something his father had said to him at the hospital, and an ironic smile came to his lips.

He saw Shelby standing there waiting for him to say something. "Come on in."

She crossed the threshold and looked around. The walls were lined with law books. There were heavy drapes at the single window. Probably very little daylight managed to get in, she mused. "I just thought you'd like a little progress report."

He put a piece of paper into the book on his desk to mark his place, and closed it. He'd done enough tonight. "Is he getting worse?"

Shelby sat down on the recliner near his desk. She shook her head at his assumption. "Why do you always have to think it has to be bad news?"

He wasn't in the mood for her perpetual good spirits. "The man has an inoperable brain tumor—"

She wouldn't let him finish. She didn't want him using his negative outlook as an excuse. "There's no need to bury him before his time," she said sharply. "As a matter of fact—" she lowered her voice again "—he's been doing rather well. He did have a minor seizure today, but I called Dr. Hemsley and he upped the dosage of phenytoin, so that should do it."

Shelby had seen concern cross Brendan's face at the mention of the seizure. So he wasn't totally divorced from his father, even though he was pretending to be. Good.

"I'll be taking your father to the hospital next Monday for another CAT scan to see if the seizure caused any damage."

Monday. The jury would be picked by then and the trial would be underway. "Need help?"

"You?" she asked in surprise. He had been distancing himself all week. The last thing she had expected was an offer of help. It confirmed her feelings that he had to be prodded, but that he really wanted to cross over that chasm he had dug between himself and his father.

"No, I thought I'd hire someone to help you...."

Disappointment twisted sharply inside her. Damn him, why did he have to be like this? Was she so wrong about him? Did she just imagine the kindness, the tenderness? No, she refused to believe that she had.

"While you're at it, why don't you hire someone to stand in for you at meals?" She got to her feet, her patience dangerously low. She had to leave. She didn't want to talk to him until her temper cooled.

He came around his desk quickly, grabbing her wrist to keep her from going. "Shelby, I'm a lawyer. I practice law. That means being in court. In law libraries. Talking to clients." Why, even when he was shouting at her, did he have this overwhelming desire to crush his mouth to hers, to forget everything and everyone but her? He really was losing it.

With effort, he struggled to hold on to his train of thought. "It doesn't leave me a hell of a whole lot of time to myself."

She pulled once, but his hand was firm on hers. Shelby gave up struggling. "No, it doesn't. It doesn't leave you time to think or to feel. Want to know what I think?"

He almost laughed. She always oversimplified things. He knew exactly what she would say. "I *know* what you think. You're Pollyanna, and think that everything can be solved with a kiss where it hurts and a few kind words." Suddenly aware that he was still holding her by the wrist, he let go. "Well, it can't."

Shelby softened. She knew she would. "Can't hurt to try."

He looked down into her face. She had no idea about these things. No idea at all. "Oh, yes, it can. It can hurt like hell."

Shelby threaded her arms around his neck and stood up on her toes so that her mouth was level with his.

"What do you think you're doing?"

Gently forcing his head down, she kissed his forehead. "Putting the first part of your theory to the test. You hurt." She tapped his head. "Up here." Her fingers trailed down to his chest. "And here." Slowly, Shelby traced the pattern of a heart.

He knew he should draw away, go back to his work. But he was trapped again. "There's no medicine for that."

How could she make him see? "Yes, there is. It's called opening up your heart." She searched his eyes for some tiny seed of communion. "He needs you."

He wished she wouldn't. He was weakening, and he didn't want to. He knew what would happen if he did. He'd already been there. "Where was he when I needed him?"

Shelby straightened to look at his face again. "I don't know. I can't answer that. All I can say is that old adage is still true. Two wrongs don't make a right. Don't be wrong, Brendan."

She asked too much of him. She always did. "Shelby—"

Shelby placed her fingers to his lips. "Please. For your own sake." He had to let his hurt heal. If he let it fester, he'd never forgive himself. He had only this small opportunity to make amends before his father died. His future peace of mind depended on it. As did their future. She was afraid of the additional pain he would suffer if he allowed the rift to go on, unresolved.

He shook his head. "I don't know if I can."

"Try," she whispered. "Try." It was an unabashed plea.

Brendan buried his hands in her hair, cupping the back of her head. Pulling her to him, he kissed her and felt alive for the first time in more than a week. It was what he had been denying himself, what he needed. His heart hammered madly as he kissed her over and over again.

Shelby felt all his pain and took it onto herself. She moaned slightly as she parted her lips. Wanting once more to soothe, she found traces of her own salvation, as well. She felt tears well up inside her. Shelby knew she loved him, loved him and saw the goodness he was denying, saw the love he kept at bay. With all her heart she wanted to bring him into awareness.

He was numb, completely numb, except for the flowering desire that was there between them. He dragged her closer to him, his hands pressing against her back, memorizing the subtle outline of her body.

He had to stop. To linger like this was only to draw out the torture. But he couldn't stop. Just a moment more. Just one second more. What did it matter when measured against all eternity?

It mattered. It helped crack the walls around him, around his heart. Until this moment, until he was filled with the wonder of her and the emotions she created within him, he had not realized just how incredibly empty he had been.

She was a temptress, yet her responses were hesitant, innocent. He could almost believe he had been her first. He knew he wanted to be her last.

Fantasies. All fantasies.

Brendan wanted just a moment longer in which to believe.

He broke away, barely able to breathe. Too fast. Everything was still spinning around too fast. He strove for something to say, holding her to him so that she couldn't see what she had done to him. "Is that the way you kiss away all the hurts?"

Shelby felt his heart hammering against her breasts. She smiled to herself. "No, just the special ones." She raised her head and looked at him. "Have you eaten?"

He thought of the pastrami sandwich the deli had delivered. That had been at one. It was eight now. "No."

She hadn't thought so. She'd been listening for him. "I kept dinner waiting for you. I haven't really eaten myself, just a little something to keep your father company." She moved to the door, then turned and held out her hand to him. "C'mon, even Super Lawyers have to eat. You can tell me all about the case over tortillas."

He could be tempted. She'd already proven that. Brendan took her hand. "No hamburgers?"

Shelby thought that over. "We can send out if you want."

He thought of the last time and shuddered. "No, I'd take my chances on your cooking."

"You're not taking any chances," she told him as Brendan turned off the light. "I happen to be a very good cook, given the opportunity. Your father thinks so."

Brendan's expression darkened just a little as he remembered. "He used to praise my mother's cooking."

"I know," she said softly. "He told me."

Brendan paused in the doorway. "You get along with him, don't you?"

"Yes. He's not a bad man. Just a weak one. A man who made a terrible mistake and who's been atoning for it all these years."

Her argument failed to convince him, although there was something within him that desperately wanted to be convinced. "He could have come back."

"He was too ashamed. He didn't think you'd forgive him."

"He was right."

She turned to look at him, searching his face for the truth. She thought that she found it. "I'm not betting the bank on that yet."

Brendan shook his head in disbelief. She just wouldn't give up, would she? ''Doesn't it ever rain on your parade?'' He could see by her determined smile that she would never let it.

''I always carry an umbrella.'' She hooked her arm through his. ''Let's get you fed, counselor.''

Food was always a safe topic for them, Brendan thought, allowing himself to be led. Nothing else seemed to be.

Chapter Thirteen

Shelby cleared away the breakfast plates and glanced at the kitchen clock. Six-thirty. It was much too early for Brendan to be leaving for the office. But this had been his routine since she had come to stay. Since his father had come to stay, she thought. That was the real reason he left so early. Because he didn't want to face his father. When would he stop running?

She turned as she heard his chair scrape against the tile floor. "Can you come home early tonight?"

Her question took him by surprise. "How early?"

"Before six." She stood with her back to the sink, waiting for an answer. She could see that she was making him uncomfortable and felt bad about it. But the situation required drastic measures.

Brendan considered his schedule. The trial, in its third week, was almost over. It had gone well. He had managed to show that all the state's evidence was nothing more than circumstantial. Barring any bombshells, and he wasn't anticipating any, the case would be turned over to the jury today.

"It could be arranged." He walked out to the foyer where he had left his briefcase. "Why?"

Shelby was determined. She kept her expression provocatively innocent as she followed him. Brendan found her particularly irresistible. He knew her well enough to anticipate that she was about to request something that he would not care for. He had to maintain his guard. "I thought you might like dinner."

The simplicity of the request made him wary that there was more to it. "I have dinner every night."

"Together."

He picked up his briefcase and then regarded her suspiciously. "Together as in how?"

You have to face this sometime, Brendan. "As in the three of us. You, me and your father."

He didn't know how much longer he could hold out against her, or against himself. The combination of guilt and her insistence was wearing him down. The fact that he felt guilty when logically he thought he shouldn't rested heavily on his mind. He had trained himself to be strong willed and disciplined. This reaction was a weakness. His father didn't deserve kindness, so why was he feeling so guilty about avoiding him? He had just cause.

"Shelby, you're my father's nurse, not his guardian angel." He pulled open the front door, then looked at her, his voice softening a little. "Don't try to fix everything all at once."

She wondered if he realized that this was the second time he had referred to Danny as his father. The term *old man* was slipping by the wayside, as was, she hoped, Brendan's animosity. Slow progress, but progress nonetheless. It reinforced her feelings that Brendan did love his father and that she was right about pushing him toward a reconciliation.

Shelby smiled up at him as she took hold of the doorknob. "Just be home before six, all right?"

"Maybe."

She took too much upon herself, Brendan thought as he walked to his car. They were going to have to have a long discussion when he returned tonight.

Nothing made Brendan feel better than when all the pieces fit neatly together, as they had in court today. He had completely destroyed the last of the state's evidence. Closing statements had almost seemed superfluous. He had seen by the D.A.'s expression that the victory was his.

As it should be, he thought.

Brendan had firmly believed in his client's innocence. He wouldn't have been able to defend him the way he had, with his last ounce of conviction, if he hadn't. He always chose his cases carefully and then became intimately involved for the space of time that was necessary to bring the case to trial. And to acquittal.

An intense, interdependent relationship would spring up and flourish for the weeks that the case was in preparation. It ended, usually well, immediately after the trial was over. Brendan never saw clients again, never got together with them socially. Quick, beneficial, intense. These were the hallmarks of all his lawyer-client relationships. And at the end, though he chose the route himself, there was always the feeling of being left alone. Again. It was a pattern he repeated, a pattern he was used to.

Today it had taken the jury only three hours to return a verdict of not guilty. His client's response had been intense disbelief and joy. Tears of relief streaming down his portly face, John Taylor Hudson had told Brendan that any favor in his power to grant was his. Brendan had merely laughed quietly and told the man that his fee would be in the mail, then sent Hudson into the waiting arms of his family, a free man.

Brendan had walked out of the courtroom alone, after the reporters had left. But this time it was different. This time he felt like celebrating. He wanted to come home to see her. To share his victory with Shelby. The novelty of the feeling frightened him a little, but he put it out of his mind.

The sound of the car in the driveway surprised her. It was too early for Brendan. It was only a little after four. Dinner wasn't anywhere nearly ready and the poker game was still going on.

"I fold," she announced, leaving her cards on the table.

"Knew she was bluffing," Murphy muttered.

Danny watched Shelby hurry from the room, wondering if Brendan had come home and if that meant that he would get a chance to see his son today. He hadn't asked for him, but he had wished.

"Shelby," Brendan called as he strode into the foyer. He dropped his briefcase on the marble table.

She hurried out and then stopped when she saw his expression. "You're grinning. Did you win?"

Overcome by something far stronger than he was, Brendan swept her into his arms and spun her around. It wasn't his first victory, but it felt like it. It was the first that he was sharing.

"I did."

She laughed, her hair flying about her shoulder as she entwined her arms around his neck. She didn't know what had brought on this burst of joy. It wasn't due to a court victory, of that she was pretty certain. But whatever it was, she was grateful to it. "Were you brilliant?"

Brendan set her down again, but didn't let go. It felt too good to hold her. "I was."

Shelby sniffed, her eyes sparkling. "Nothing less than I expected."

He wanted to make love with her, here, now, in the middle of the day, in the middle of the house. He settled for just holding her. "Are you always so accurate?"

"Every time." Shelby took a step backward, looking over her shoulder toward the dining room. "C'mon, there's someone I'd like you to meet. Actually, two someones."

A little of the elation faded. "Who?"

She saw the change and refused to let it penetrate the euphoria he had created. "Come with me and you'll find out."

She took his arm and almost pulled him into the dining room. He found his father there, sitting in his wheelchair. Instead of the robe he expected to see the man wearing, Danny was fully dressed in a light blue velour pullover and light gray slacks. He looked as if he anticipated getting out of his wheelchair at any moment. He appeared far readier for life than for death. Though still thin and fragile, he now had some of the old vitality that Brendan associated with the memory of his father.

There were two other men at the table. Young, wide-shouldered, strapping men who looked as if they could be used for a marine recruiting poster, except that their dark hair was on the long side.

Brendan looked quizzically at Shelby.

"Brendan, I'd like you to meet my brothers, Tyler and Murphy." She gestured from one man to the other.

"I'm Murphy," the one closest to Brendan said, rising in his seat as he shook Brendan's hand.

"That makes me Tyler," the other told him. As soon as Murphy released Brendan's hand, Tyler grasped it warmly and shook it as if it mattered.

Brendan looked from one to the other, slightly bewildered. What were they doing here?

"And they both cheat at cards," Danny added.

"If anyone's cheating," Tyler said to the older man, seating himself again, "it's you." He indicated the large pile of matchsticks next to Danny's hand. "Hasn't anyone ever taught you it's dangerous to cheat a policeman?"

"You're a policeman?" Brendan asked.

"Yeah," Tyler responded. "And you're one hell of a lawyer." There was genuine admiration evident in Tyler's voice. "Read about the trial in the newspaper last night." He shook his head for emphasis. "If I'm ever in trouble, I want you on my side."

"I'll take that as a retainer," Brendan said, crossing toward the doorway. "Shelby." He nodded at her. "Can I see you a minute?"

Shelby wondered if he was annoyed. She hadn't asked him if her brothers could come over to play cards, and it was his house. But she saw no harm in providing Danny with people to socialize with and something to do with his hours. After all, Brendan didn't make any effort to keep the man company when he was home.

"Yes?" The dining-room door closed behind them. Shelby kept her back against it, bracing herself.

Brendan turned to look at her. A strange sort of anger filtered through him. He couldn't put his finger on its source. "Why are they here?"

"To lose at poker, apparently," she said lightly, hoping to distract his annoyance. "Your father is one deuce of a poker player. A hundred years ago he could have made a living on a river boat as a gambler."

"Probably something he tried along the way and failed at," he muttered, a trace of bitterness in his voice. "You still haven't answered my question."

She raised her chin. It wasn't exactly a defensive gesture. It was more as if she was taking a stand. "Is this what's called relentless cross-examination?"

He crossed his arms as he leveled a gaze at her, waiting. "No, this is what's called trying to get a straight answer."

Shelby shrugged. "It's their day off. Your father was lonely and they all like to play poker. I just mixed them together. It's not the first time." She stopped and looked at him. "Are you angry?"

Was he angry about his father enjoying himself with other people? Maybe. No, he didn't think so, but he honestly couldn't answer that. He addressed himself to the fact that strangers were present in his house. "No, it's just that I would have liked to have been told."

Shelby turned toward the kitchen. She still hadn't seen to dinner. "Consider yourself told."

Brendan put his hands on the door, stopping her from leaving. There were times when she could be utterly infuriating. "Ahead of time."

"Next time I'll call you." She forgot about dinner as she turned again and looked at him closely. "You're not annoyed that they're here."

There she went again, sounding so sure of herself. "What makes you say that?"

"Because I've gotten to know you." *Know you better than you want me to know you,* she added silently. Brendan, she saw, was feeling left out. "Do you play poker?"

"Some." He didn't add that his father had taught him. It had been years since he had held a deck in his hands.

"A novice. Oh, they'll love you." Before he could protest, she took his hand and brought him back to the dining room.

"Shelby, no, I—"

"Have something more important to do?" she second-guessed, her voice low. "No, I don't think so." Nothing was more important than sitting down with his father. "At least give it a try for a hand or two. Please." It would do him so much good, she thought. They had to reconcile. For everyone's sake.

She turned toward the others at the table. "I'm officially dropping out."

"Coward," Murphy accused.

"But—" she held up a finger "—I have another pigeon for you. Player, if you prefer." She nodded at Brendan.

Tyler gestured toward Shelby's empty chair. "Make yourself at home, counselor."

"I am at home," Brendan pointed out and then saw that Shelby was grinning at him. It took him a moment to understand why. He had referred to this as home. He never had before. It was a technical slip of the tongue, he told himself, nothing more than that.

"Okay," he said as he took off his jacket and slung it over the back of his chair, "what are the rules?"

Shelby slipped into the kitchen. Sandwiches would be in order, she decided. Nobody looked as if they really wanted to stop for a regular dinner. It was, she had a feeling, going to be a long night.

"I had no idea so much time had passed," Brendan said to Shelby as the front door closed on her departing brothers. He followed her into the dining room. Danny had already gone to bed and it was just the two of them now. He liked the sound of that.

Shelby began to gather the empty plates that were left in the wake of the game. Brendan followed, collecting empty and half-empty glasses. "That's what happens when you get caught up in something." She stacked the plates together. "Are you always so determined to win?"

He shrugged, not understanding why she would even bother to ask. "Why play if you don't want to win?"

Shelby laughed. There was so much he still had to learn. So much he needed to be able to see. "For the company. To pass the time. To learn about the other person." She stopped and cocked her head in his direction. "Shall I go on?"

"If I say no, will you stop?" He knew better than that.

She glanced at her watch. It was a quarter to ten. Even live-ins had hours. "I'm still in your employ for another fifteen minutes, so I guess I'd have to."

Brendan set the glasses back down on the table, intrigued. "You mean for the next fifteen minutes you have to do anything I say?" He led her to the living room. She saw the glint in his eyes. A thrill passed over her. "Anything," she answered solemnly.

"Come here."

It was all she wanted to hear. Shelby melted into his arms. "Gladly."

His lips lowered to hers. There was still hunger in his kiss, and an unquenched desire that had gone begging for the past week. But he took his time in kissing her, as if savoring the taste and feel of her and letting all his senses drink it in. He would never have his fill, no matter how hard he tried, no matter how much he lied to himself and said that he would.

His kiss deepened and he fell in.

It was amazing how drunk she could become on him. All he had to do was hold her and it started. She put her arms around his neck, threading her fingers together as if to secure herself to something tangible as she went spinning off into space.

She loved him, loved him so much that it hurt. But it was a sweet pain. It wasn't anything like the one she knew that he was enduring. The pain she was determined to help him heal.

Just as she thought that she was lost forever, Brendan moved back. Involuntarily she moaned a little.

"I think," she said, her voice low to keep it from quivering as their lips drew apart, "that you were the big winner tonight."

He shook his head. She had her facts wrong. "My father had most of the matchsticks."

Unwilling to step back, she kept her arms around his neck. "Yes, but you were still the big winner."

He smiled. "Not very subtle, are you?"

"At times. When it works." She feathered her fingers through his hair. It was thick and soft. Just touching him made her want. "At other times, I find two-by-fours come in handy."

He laughed and hugged her to him. "What would you like to use on me?"

She grinned. That was easy. "Something soft."

He could feel himself responding to her, to the sight and the scent of her, just by standing here, bantering. "Like?"

She rose on her toes, her lips inches from his again. "Guess."

Her breath on his face excited him. He ran his hands slowly along her body, wanting her to feel the same excitement, the same edginess that possessed him. He saw desire flicker in her eyes and knew he was succeeding. "What do I get if I guess right?"

The throbbing was beginning, starting at the core, making her moist, making her yearn. "A prize."

He kept stroking her, sliding his hands along her buttocks, molding her to him. He nipped at her lower lip. She moaned. "Can I pick it?"

Shelby's breathing was audible. "Only if you make the right choice."

Slowly, with just the tip of his tongue, he outlined her lips. Shelby felt her knees weakening. Everything was turning to liquid within her—hot, flaming liquid.

"No pressure, huh?" Brendan teased.

She shook her head, or thought she did. Her head was swimming. "None whatsoever."

Even now, with desire consuming every inch of him, Brendan couldn't help but laugh. "Shelby, you're incredible."

So are you, she thought, her mind fogging. "It's included in the price. Talk fast, you only have another twelve minutes."

He played with the top button of her blouse, worrying it in and out of the hole, making her crazy as his fingers brushed against her breasts. "What I have in mind," Brendan told her, "is going to take a lot longer than twelve minutes."

She wanted to rip his expensive, custom-tailored shirt off his back. She wanted to feel his skin pressed against her naked breasts. And she could see in his eyes that he knew it. She didn't care. She had never believed in playing games.

"Then I guess we'd better get started," she murmured, her voice husky and low with desire.

"That's the best suggestion you've had all day." He kissed the hollow of her throat, making a thousand different points of light explode within her head. "But I've got better ones."

Shelby dug her fingers into his shoulders as he pulled her blouse out and reached up beneath the material, finding her warm and wanting. "I can't wait to hear them."

He was afraid of the emotion that was taking hold of him, afraid because he thought he recognized it and knew that it had no future. And yet he didn't want to let it go. Not yet, not now. If he didn't give a name to it, then maybe it would stay. Maybe he could savor it just a little before it turned to dust.

He moved slowly, his body in tune with hers, responding to every soft curve. "Are you sure this is covered in your sister's instruction manual?"

Hungrily Shelby pressed her lips to his, her tongue darting hesitantly in, then touching his. She moaned again, then pulled away to catch her breath. She wound her fingers in his shirt, dazed. "If it's not, I'll add a footnote."

He stroked her hair, sifting it through his fingers. "I thought about you today."

She drew back her head to look at him. It took a moment to focus. "Tell me."

He kissed each eye. The flutter of her dark lashes tickled. And teased. "Tell you what?"

She couldn't wrap her arms around him any tighter, yet she tried, wanting to absorb him, to keep a piece of him with her always. "When you thought about me."

He took a breath, needing to clear his senses of her for just a moment.

"I was in the middle of my summation to the jury. The woman in the back row had red hair and it made me think of you, right in the middle of the crucial part." He remembered that he had almost lost the thread of his sentence. It made him realize how strong Shelby's hold on him was.

She shook her head, her hair brushing against his face. It excited him. "I don't have red hair."

"Then what is it?"

"Auburn."

He held up a strand, as if to examine it. What he really wanted was to examine her, inch by sensuous inch, all night long. "Looks red to me."

She watched his eyes. They were dark and smoky. "Do you like it?"

"Yes," he whispered, kissing the side of her neck. "Very much."

It took effort to remember the subject. "Then it's red." She felt his laugh ripple against the sensitive area of her skin. His fingers were beneath her blouse again, touching, massaging, creating havoc.

"You're easy," he told her.

Shelby braced her hands on his shoulders. "Only with you." She laughed, her words warm and sexy against his mouth. "Only with you."

The last button was released. Her blouse hung open. "How easy?"

She straightened slightly, her breasts thrust forward, inviting. "Why don't you find that out for yourself?"

The words were playful. The sensations that crackled between them were not.

He turned and looked at the fire that rose in the fireplace. This time she had started it. In the hearth and within him. "I don't know why they call this a conversation pit. No conversation is ever completed here."

Determined to create havoc of her own, Shelby hooked her fingertips along his waistband, slowly rimming it, pressing against his skin. Teasing him. "Maybe they should call it a starter pit."

He jerked as her fingers dipped low, caressing him. Only extreme restraint kept Brendan from taking her here. "Maybe."

His mouth closed over hers. Tongues tangled, emotions erupted, until they were both breathless from wanting, from anticipating.

"Why don't we go upstairs and finish this conversation properly?" he said to her.

"Another good suggestion." She ran her tongue along her lips, tasting him. "Counselor, I do believe that you're on a roll."

He drew her to him, his arm around her shoulders as they crossed to the staircase. Above, the chandelier glistened like so many stars.

"Not yet, but give me time."

Shelby rested her hand on his chest as they went up the stairs side by side. "You can have all the time in the world."

Chapter Fourteen

Brendan knew he hadn't a prayer tonight. The more he resisted, the more he found himself entrenched. Resistance was for the strong who could entertain some small hope of winning. Tomorrow, when the sun was shining brightly, when logic was once more present and paths clearly defined, he would again tell himself why he couldn't let this happen, why he couldn't surrender to feelings—especially those that were spun out of threads so thin they seemed to be totally invisible, yet so strong that there was no breaking them once they were wound around him.

But that was tomorrow. For now, all he wanted was to hold her, to kiss her, to stop being Brendan Connery and just be.

She had tasted the hunger in his first kiss and knew that their lovemaking was going to be just as it had been before: wild, reckless, all consuming. And wondrous beyond her wildest dreams. There was something here, in the urgency of his kiss, in the heat of his hands as they roamed her body, that she had never experienced before on any level. Something sweeter, something darker and more dangerous. Something she knew that, once sampled, she could never do without again.

There was more here than just body meeting body, more than lips caressing lips, or hands touching secret places and evoking waves of passionate desire. Though that would have been enough, though the power of the physical responses that racked her body were more than she could ever have believed possible, there was more. So very much more.

There was love, unspoken but alive.

And it was that that took her heart prisoner, that totally burned away any hope of Shelby's ever escaping its far-reaching power.

Nor did she want any.

"What kept you?" she murmured as he shut the bedroom door behind them.

He took her into his arms again, wanting to make love with her immediately, wanting to draw it out all night. He wanted it all and he wanted it with her.

He thought she was confused. "I came home early," he reminded her.

Her entire body felt fluid, pouring into his arms. "Not early, late. Six days late." It had been six long days since he had so much as kissed her. She slid her hands up his arms, around his neck. "Oh, Brendan, you are a stubborn man."

He pushed her blouse from her shoulders, kissing each one in turn. Her skin was cool. It fanned the flames that much more. Lightly he burned a trail up her throat to her mouth. "I've done all the talking today that I'm going to."

She grinned against his lips, transferring her smile to him. "Fine with me."

The jeans she had worn were banished to the floor in a heap, joining her blouse. Brendan's fingers tangled in her teddy, slowly working her body and her passions free at the same time, until that flimsy garment, too, whispered down to the floor.

"Did you forget something?" she prompted softly.

"I forget nothing," he answered, stripping off his clothing. He did it in between assaulting her lips with kisses that grew more and more intense.

Shelby worked to help free him of his clothing, her urgency heightening his. Their clothes tangled and so did they, hopelessly, tantalizingly. The feel of his body against hers seemed so preciously natural to her. Shelby felt as if it had always been this way. As if she had been his since the very beginning, before time could be measured.

Shelby fought to curb the eager rush of excitement that shot through her, the mad, pounding desire to reach the summits quickly. She dug her fingers into his back. She felt the muscles ripple beneath her hand. She felt him shudder as her fingers probed lower. Shudder for her.

The power she felt, the power she had, excited her and held her in awe at the same time. But foremost were the sensations of exquisite agony passing through her like a shower of needles as his mouth lightly skimmed over all the sensitive areas of her body.

Lightly, Brendan's tongue glided along her breast, making her nipple rise taut and ready. Shelby arched her body as his hands replaced his mouth and he forged lower, deeper, brushing along her navel until her stomach quivered of its own volition with burning expectations.

Wave after wave of heightening desire, of pleasures nearly peaking, consumed her and still he moved lower, his lips circling the most sensitive area of all until he plunged his tongue in, taking what she wanted so badly to give.

Shelby twisted and turned, unable to keep herself still. She pressed her lips together as hard as she could to keep from crying out, grabbed fistfuls of bedclothes to keep from snatching and clawing at Brendan as her body was sent hurtling over peak after peak. She wanted him to stop, for the bittersweet agony she felt was too much to withstand. Yet she wanted him to go on forever.

Breathing heavily, her lungs unable to sustain enough air to steady her racing pulse, Shelby wordlessly urged Brendan upward until the length of his body was stretched over hers. Until his lips were on hers again.

Brendan had completely lost himself in the worship of her body, so taut, so ready, so perfectly his. When she kissed him now his desire was so strong that he was afraid he would never regain any footing. He was the slave and she the master, of his body, of his mind, of his very soul.

And then the roles reversed, spinning round and round until nothing was clearly defined anymore.

There was no give-and-take any longer, only sharing, pleasing and desire at once so savage and yet tender that it overwhelmed both of them.

Wherever life took him, whatever lot it chose to cast for him, he would always have this one night, Brendan thought just before they went over the edge together. And it would sustain him.

* * *

When he awoke the next morning, the first thing that flashed into his consciousness was Shelby and the night they had shared. He felt his limbs warm as the memory came flooding back to him.

The next thing he became aware of was that there was something tied to his wrist. He raised his left hand and realized that there was a handkerchief tied to it. A handkerchief that was joined to two others before it was linked to the one that was tied to Shelby's wrist. Brendan stared at it for a long moment, not knowing what to think. Shaking his head, he began to untie it, fumbling at the knot. It held firm. The woman was a regular Boy Scout. What had possessed her to do this?

His struggling woke Shelby, just as it had been intended to.

"Hi," she murmured, rubbing the sleep from her eyes with her free hand. She sat up, her hair tousled from her night's sleep, tumbled all around her shoulders. It was the color of the sun as it rose in the sky.

She made his mouth water, looking the way she did. But there were other matters to settle first. He held up his wrist. "What's this?"

"A handkerchief. Several, actually." She dragged her free hand through her hair, trying to come to. It always took her a few moments. "I found them in your top drawer." She pointed over to the bureau and yanked his hand along with hers.

"I know what they are. I want to know what they are doing knotted together and on my wrist?" He raised his wrist again for emphasis, still baffled.

"I didn't want to wake up alone again." She smiled at him sweetly, negating any excuses he might have to offer about that, or any annoyance he might try to hide behind. "I figured that if you tried to untie yourself, I'd wake up. I used four so that you'd have some freedom moving around."

"Very considerate of you." The odd logic of it as well as the absurdity had him laughing. He finished untying the one on his wrist.

"I try, Brendan. I try very hard." She held up her wrist for him to do next.

Brendan obliged, noting that her sheet was slipping. "This looks like a variation of bondage."

"It isn't." She tossed the linked handkerchiefs to the floor on the other side of the bed. "Physical bonds aren't necessary." She smiled as she lightly ran the tip of her fingers along his chest. "The other kind are much stronger."

He turned in bed to look at her as she sat there, a sheet just barely tucked around her small breasts, the rest of her deliciously, temptingly nude beneath the covers. He felt his body tighten, ready.

"What other kind?"

She didn't answer. Instead, she leaned over and lightly kissed him on the lips. Her hair tumbled down farther, like a wave of red gold sea, brushing against his bare shoulder, tantalizing him.

It was all the encouragement he needed.

"C'mere, you." He slid back into the bed, dragging her to him until she was on top.

"I just love Saturdays, don't you?" she murmured against his mouth, framing it with tiny kisses that completely dissolved any control he might have left.

He ran his hands along her hips, resting them on her buttocks. "They never seemed to matter before," he answered honestly. Nothing ever seemed to matter before there was Shelby.

"That just may change." Shelby laughed, wiggling into place against him. She felt his body hardening beneath her. Her grin widened.

He wanted her, wanted that wild rush that only she provided. He filled his hands with her hair, bringing her mouth down to his.

"Maybe," he agreed.

She almost sighed for the pleasure it evoked. "You're a hard man to convince." Her body teased him.

He bracketed her face with his hands again as he kissed her hard. "Convince me...."

When he came down for breakfast two hours later, his hair still damp from his shower, Brendan was surprised to find his father at the kitchen table. Awkwardness immediately seeped in.

Shelby saw the look on Brendan's face as she turned to place his omelet on the table. Oh, no, he wasn't retreating. Not from either of them.

"I thought," she said quickly, keeping her voice even, "that since it was Saturday, and you didn't have to go to the office—"

"I—" Brendan began to fabricate an excuse. There were things he could be doing at his office. There were always things to be done, other cases to consider. But there was nothing there that couldn't wait until Monday morning.

She wasn't going to let him dodge this any longer. "That we could have a nice breakfast together, I mean." She glanced at Danny's hopeful expression and continued hurriedly. "Seeing as how last night went so well."

"Last night?" Brendan echoed, confused. What did their lovemaking have to do with eating breakfast with his father?

She poured a glass of orange juice for him and placed it on the table. "The poker game." The smile she fought to restrain was barely restricted to her eyes.

"Oh, right, the poker game." Brendan passed his hand over his face, gathering his thoughts. Since he was already down here, and faced with this, he might as well try, he supposed.

He sat down at the table. Shelby looked at him, encouragement in her eyes. "You play rather well," he told his father.

"Just luck." Danny passed it off, but the compliment, however small, literally made him glow.

Brendan raised his eyes to regard the man sitting opposite him. It suddenly dawned on him that his father was hungry, hungry for his approval, for his attention. For his forgiveness. The roles, it appeared, had reversed themselves.

He had been hungry once, too, Brendan thought, bitterness rising. Hungry for his father's love. It was hard to forget that. Or to forgive.

Shelby sat down next to Brendan and saw the shield rising again. "Since your father's doing so well," she interjected, "I thought perhaps you'd both like to come." She began buttering her toast nonchalantly.

As usual, she had lost him. Brendan set his coffee cup down. "To what?"

She looked from one man to the other. "My cousin Eileen just had a baby."

"Congratulations," Brendan said dryly, but he knew it wasn't going to end here. Nothing ever did with her. His curiosity was aroused.

Shelby leaned toward him. She was getting ready for the kill, he thought, amused at how well he had come to know her habits. "There's a christening party today at three. I thought—'' she looked at Danny and smiled ''—that being around people might be good for your father's spirits.''

He was going to play this out as long as he could. Besides, he really had no interest in getting involved in this. ''Fine, then you go with my blessings.''

Brendan began to pick up the newspaper that she had left by his plate. He didn't get to read beyond the first three words of the headline. Shelby's hand was on his arm, stopping him.

''I'd like you to come, too.''

He knew he shouldn't look at her face, but he did. And was lost. ''Why?''

She shrugged helplessly. ''I need help with the wheelchair.''

He narrowed his eyes. The lie was flimsy, to say the least. ''Since when do you need help?''

''Since now.'' She leaned on her upturned hand. She heard Danny chuckling into his coffee in the background, but she continued looking at Brendan, daring him to turn her down.

This was his self-preservation they were bandying about. Brendan had every intention of turning her down. He didn't fit in with family gatherings. He was the odd man out. He had always been odd man out. Because of his father. Even his mother's family had turned their backs on him after she had died.

No, he wasn't going. There was no point in even discussing the matter.

''When did you say it was?'' The voice belonged to him, but he had no idea what possessed him to ask.

Shelby brightened, relieved. There had been a moment there when she had thought she had lost him. ''Three o'clock, if that's all right with you.''

"No," he retorted. At least this much he was allowed, Brendan thought. "It's not all right with me." He saw her brow wrinkle and rise beneath the wave of auburn. "But I'll come."

"That's all I ask." Shelby rose, kissing his temple. She was finished with her toast.

"No, that's not all you ask," he murmured under his breath. "You're asking for a hell of a lot more than that."

She wasn't going to be drawn in to any kind of negative discussion, not when she felt so good, not when the sun was shining so brightly outside and all was well with the world. "One step at a time, Brendan, just one tiny step at a time."

She passed Danny as she made her way to the sink, and winked at him.

The old man would have kissed her if he could.

Brendan stood on the outskirts of the huge backyard, looking around slowly. If there was grass, it was hard to see. There were people literally covering every square inch of the area.

"This is your family?" He looked at Shelby, stunned. How could anyone have so many relatives and keep track of them?

She nodded. "Some of them. Move, Brendan, you're blocking the way." Shelby urged him into the yard.

Brendan scarcely realized that he was pushing his father before him as he moved farther into the yard. "Some of them?" he echoed. "My God, this looks like a production of The Waltons Meet the Brady Bunch."

She grinned, taking over for him. He surrendered the wheelchair readily. "I warned you."

"When?" He looked at her incredulously. "When did you warn me?"

Her eyes teased him. "When you helped me with the food cart the day you met me. I said, 'Be careful.'"

He laughed, his self-consciousness abating. "And that was supposed to cover everything?"

She merely grinned at him, her eyes dancing. "I don't like to repeat myself."

"Ha!"

If he thought that he and his father wouldn't fit in, that they would be shut out by this overzealous family unit, he was not prepared for Shelby's family. Tyler was the first to see them arriving. He spotted them before they even had a chance to cross five feet into the yard. The hearty policeman dragged Murphy, still clutching a piece of cake, with him and greeted Brendan and Danny as if they were old friends. Introductions to their wives, Katie and Elizabeth, were quickly forthcoming. Irene and Patsy with their husbands and children were next. Brendan's head swam with names and faces.

The din at the party quickly became overwhelming. Brendan turned to Shelby and asked, "Did everyone in your family overdose on sugar when they were children?"

She inclined her head toward his. "No," she answered in the same tone. "Just on love."

He shoved his hands into his pockets. "I wouldn't know about that."

"No, maybe not, but you will," she promised. "You will. Come," she coaxed, raising her voice above the din, "there's someone here I'd like you to meet. Make yourself useful, Tyler," she said to her brother over her shoulder. "Push the wheelchair."

Though Brendan knew that his best bet was to turn around and go back to the car now, while he still had a chance, he found himself doing as she asked and following Shelby deeper into this land of Oz she was bringing him to. With Murphy, Tyler and the others closing ranks behind him and talking to him nonstop, there wasn't much else that he really could do.

Or, he found, that he wanted to.

Chapter Fifteen

Even if Brendan had tried to hang back at this gathering of exuberant relations, no one would have let him. He was accepted and made to feel as if he were part of the family almost immediately. And, in an odd sort of way, he who had always dwelled on the fringe of things, separated both mentally and emotionally if not actually physically, actually *wanted* to be pulled into this bosom of a thriving family.

Perhaps not completely on a conscious level. He had buried his needs too deeply for it to be a conscious desire. Consciously he made every effort to stand away from the crowd, although that wasn't easy. The ocean of people kept swelling and changing shape and somehow encompassing Brendan no matter where he stood. A child wanted to play catch with him. An adult, recognizing him from a newspaper photograph, wanted to offer a few choice words of congratulations, or pose a question. Brendan found himself checkmated each way he turned. He could not be alone in a crowd here. No one allowed it.

Making good his escape from a group of older women who were inquiring as to his marital status, he walked headlong into a brightly attired young woman who was obviously in a hurry. She handed him her baby to hold as if he was an old and trusted friend.

"I'll only be a minute, Patrick," she promised breathlessly as she hurried away.

"But I'm not Patrick." His words fell on deaf ears as the woman rushed off into the house.

Brendan stared down incredulously at the squirming bundle in his arms. It was drooling. Now what was he supposed to do with this? Brendan looked around, desperately searching for any one of a number of people he had been introduced to. Preferably, he wanted Shelby, but at the moment he wasn't going to be fussy.

Shelby found him.

"Hi." She came up from behind and peered at the baby he held so awkwardly before him. "I saw your look of abject distress." She dug into her purse for a tissue and dabbed it at the stain on his shirt.

Brendan had always liked to believe that he was up to any given situation. That faith was leaving him. "It's not distress." The baby yelped and he shifted his hold. He had absolutely no idea how to hold a wiggling infant. "It's just that I've never held one of these things before."

Shelby grinned but made absolutely no effort to relieve him of his burden. She was enjoying this. "It shows."

He muttered something short and sharp under his breath as he looked around for the baby's mother. She was wearing a bright orange dress. He couldn't find a single trace of her in the sea of humanity that was ebbing and flowing around him.

"Some woman just handed it to me," he told Shelby in disbelief.

Shelby nodded, apparently, he thought, taking this sort of behavior in stride. "Alba."

"Who?"

"Alba," she repeated. "That's Alba's baby." She tickled the baby under the chin.

Babies all looked alike to Brendan. He had no idea how she could tell whose this was. "Is she always so careless?"

Shelby stopped tickling and cooing at the baby. "Excuse me?"

He tried to keep the impatience out of his voice. He wanted Shelby to take the child, but he wasn't about to ask her. "About who watches her child?" he elaborated.

He still didn't get it, she thought. But he would, in time. "Trusting. The word is *trusting*. This is a family gathering. Besides, she probably mistook you for someone."

The baby had grabbed his shirt and was beginning to suck on it rather avidly. He wondered when it was fed last. "She did call me Patrick."

Shelby tugged the fabric out of the baby's mouth. A large wet spot emerged, feeling clammy against his chest. With a cry of protest, the baby grabbed the shirt back.

Shelby looked at Brendan closely, studying for a moment. "There is a small resemblance. Except Patrick smiles a lot more. He's my cousin." She looked around at the large gathering. "One of many."

"Yes, so I see." Juggling the baby, Brendan separated it from his shirt again. "What is it?" he asked, holding the baby at arm's length and looking down into the sunny face.

Shelby laughed. He looked adorable in his distress. "Can't you tell?"

"How can I tell?" He held the baby up higher to illustrate his point. "It's dressed in yellow. Yellow's a neutral color."

"I thought maybe the way that Martha was looking at you with those adoring eyes might be a clue." Shelby's own eyes, he noted, were filled with amusement at his plight.

"Are you trying to flatter me?"

"Yes, and obviously failing." She decided it was time to put him out of his misery. "Want me to take her?"

He'd thought she'd never ask. "With pleasure." He extended Martha to her as if he was handing over a bundle of wet laundry.

Shelby raised her hands up, fingers pointing skyward, avoiding contact at the last minute. "Although you looked kind of sweet, holding her."

He glared at her as he thrust the child forward. Shelby took Martha with a laugh. "Just how many *are* there in your family?"

Settling Martha against her shoulder, oblivious to the sucking motion, Shelby looked around. "No one's really counting, what with the marriages and births going on. Mom and Dad each came from large families."

He watched Martha in mounting fascination. The baby was trying to suck up Shelby's dress, starting from her left shoulder. "And propagated one of their own."

"Yes, I guess five is a big number, at least these days."
She looked at his profile, trying to discern what he was
thinking. "How do you like it?"

Brendan looked back at her, puzzled. "How do I like
what?"

She gestured with her head since her arms were full.
"Being in a large family."

"I'm not in it," he pointed out. Fruitlessly, probably, he thought.

"Physically, then," she amended. "You are standing
here and Alba did mistake you for a relative, so, for all
intents and purposes, you can be in one for the day. No
one'll penalize you, I promise."

He didn't answer her question. If he told her that it
was all right, she'd probably take it as a four-star en-
dorsement. Instead, he nodded at the baby. "Doesn't
anyone feed that kid?"

"She's teething."

"That would explain the drool marks."

Brendan looked around again, wondering if the
baby's mother was ever going to reappear. Trusting.
Shelby had said it was a matter of trust. He wondered
what it would be like to be in the midst of a group of
people whom he trusted, people who inherently trusted
him. Nice, he decided. It might be nice.

But it wasn't something he was ever going to find out
firsthand.

He wondered where his father was. He realized that he
hadn't really seen the man since Murphy had wheeled
him away to meet Shelby's parents. That had been over
an hour ago. When Shelby had taken Brendan over to
meet the couple who were, in part, responsible for all
this, his father wasn't there.

He finally spotted Danny at the far end of the yard. Instead of looking worn and tired, the way he had when Brendan had first seen him in the hospital, there was a glow in his face. For a moment Brendan had to remind himself that the man was gravely ill. He didn't look it, not anymore. A ring of children was gathered around the old man and he seemed to be the center of attention, happily holding court.

"He's telling stories," Brendan said quietly, as if to himself. He remembered his father's stories, remembered being mesmerized as pictures would form in his mind, vividly painted because of Danny's gift of making the most mundane things come alive.

Shifting the baby to her other shoulder, Shelby looked over toward the circle of children. "He seems to be quite a hit."

"Yeah, he's a kid himself, I guess." Brendan shrugged looking away. "That's part of his charm."

She heard the slight touch of bitterness in his voice. She also heard the trace of wistfulness, as if Brendan wished he could be a child again, and believe in the man who sat there spinning stories.

Still holding Martha, Shelby managed to thread an arm through his. Brendan looked at her quizzically. "You must have loved him very much."

"I—" He began to deny it, vehemently. But there was no use, not with her. She seemed to be an expert on the subject. An expert, it would seem, on him. "Yeah," he said flatly, "I did."

He didn't fool her and she was beginning to believe that he wasn't fooling himself, either. "I think you still do."

"Love can die," he said evenly, looking away from her.

"It doesn't necessarily die. Sometimes it just goes to sleep for a while." She tugged on his arm. "C'mon."

"Where are we going now?" He thought that she was going to drag him over toward his father, but she was leading him in the opposite direction.

"You haven't had any cake yet."

He relaxed a little and nodded toward the baby. "What if Alba comes back?"

"She'll find us," Shelby assured him. "Here." She handed Martha to him. Caught off guard, he took the baby. "You hold Martha. She seems only to have eyes for you, anyway." She began to lead the way.

"Shelby," he called after her urgently, then caught up in a couple of strides. "I'm not any good at this."

She turned and laughed. "Sure you are. Look." She gestured toward him. "You've gone from holding her as if she were wet laundry to holding her as if she was breakable. It's coming to you."

"What's coming to me," he said as he followed Shelby, weaving his way through the crowd and noticing the way people kept smiling at him, "is that I stand very little chance against you."

She looked over her shoulders, amused. "Very little chance?" she repeated. "Counselor, where I'm concerned, you don't have a prayer. The cake's this way."

She brought him over to a canopied area of the yard that had been set up to help feed the multitude that had gathered. Gallons of punch were still there, unconsumed. Part of a cake that had once been in the shape of a huge white stork stood in the center of the long table.

"There's still plenty left," Shelby told him. "They all cook as if it's for an army."

"It *is* an army," Brendan muttered. He took out his keys and jingled them in front of the baby. Martha cooed in excitement and tried to eat them.

Shelby turned, the plate with a piece of cake on it in her hand, and then smiled at the scene. The cake, she decided, could wait.

"An amusement park?" It seemed to Brendan that a Saturday morning didn't go by without another outing proposed by Shelby.

"It'll be fun," she promised, settling next to him on the sofa. "Which one's your favorite?"

Brendan put down the newspaper he had been trying to read. "I don't have a favorite."

Shelby sat on the sofa next to him, tucking her feet under herself. "You must have liked one over another when you went," she pressed.

"I never went."

Shelby's enthusiasm came to a skidding halt. Something else she didn't know about him. No one had ever bothered entertaining him, even in the simplest of ways. He heart went out to him, brimming with love, wanting to fix it all for him. There were so many things she wanted to say, to do. She wanted to hold him, to tell him that somehow she'd give him back the years he had lost.

But she knew she couldn't. She couldn't say it because it would embarrass him and she couldn't give him back any of the time he had lost. She could only give him the present.

And the future, if he let her.

Shelby made up her mind. "Then it's high time you and your father went."

Like all her other ideas, this one seemed off the wall to him at the outset. He was too old for amusement parks. "Shelby, I don't know."

"That's what you said about the christening," she reminded him. "You survived that, didn't you?"

He was beginning to relent. He knew he would. "Just barely."

She patted his knee, every inch the patient nurse. "This is good for you."

He doubted it. "You're my father's nurse, not mine."

Shelby rose. As far as she was concerned, it was settled. "Of course not. Then I'd charge double." She grinned, extending her hand to him. "Get up. I'll need help."

He wrapped his fingers around hers, because he needed to. Touching her had become as necessary to him as breathing. And almost as unconsciously involuntary. "I don't think you're the one who's going to be needing it."

She looked up into his face. "Just who'd you have in mind?"

He couldn't resist temptation very well anymore. He kissed her lightly. Anything more and they would never leave the living room. "Me."

Shelby cocked her head, regarding him playfully. "Anyone ever tell you that you're a big baby?"

"Never." He followed as she walked out of the room.

"Then you'll be mine." Shelby stopped at the stairs. She had to get Danny ready. "Change into something comfortable and we'll get started."

He stood, his hand on the banister, wondering what made someone like Shelby tick. "How do I get the word *no* across to you?"

"You don't. Just be glad I'm not on one of your juries," she tossed over her shoulder as she disappeared behind the staircase.

"Every day, Shelby," he answered, walking up the stairs. "Every single day."

Brendan decided that he would suffer through the trip to the park patiently. He was wrong. He didn't suffer at all. He enjoyed it, completely against his will, the way he enjoyed having Shelby in his life.

Shelby had chosen Knotts Berry Farm for its shows and its emphasis on western motifs. She had chosen well. Danny was like a child, not knowing where to look first, enjoying everything. They attended the Birdcage Theater where they watched an old-fashioned melodrama. Audience participation was encouraged and they booed the villain and cheered the hero. Or at least, Shelby thought, glancing at Brendan, two of them did. Brendan sat and watched in silence. But miracles, Shelby believed, took time.

They saw the Wild West Stunt Show, ate cotton candy near the Roaring Twenties display and took in everything the park had to offer.

"What *is* this stuff?" Brendan asked Shelby as he chewed his way around the white paper cone.

"Cotton candy," she repeated.

"No, really. What's it made of?" His father, he saw, had already finished his.

"Sugar, air, fairy tales and dreams," she answered, handing him a paper napkin.

"Not very scientific."

"No, but very good. Chin," she prompted, then took the napkin from him and did the honors herself.

It would have been a glimpse of missed childhood, if he didn't want her so.

Though he was weak, Danny could take a few steps and insisted on riding the stagecoach. With Shelby and Brendan on either side, he boarded the coach and enjoyed himself royally. The ride on the train with its choreographed robbery seemed almost anticlimactic.

Danny wanted to do everything. It was hard to determine who was having more fun, though the senior Connery made no bones about showing his enthusiasm. Brendan tried to contain his enjoyment. But Shelby could tell he was having a good time.

They wandered around the park and took in all the sights twice. They came to a halt by the log ride. Danny looked at it wistfully, but he wasn't up to it. Shelby gently pointed that out.

"But you are," Brendan guessed.

"How can you tell?" Shelby parked Danny's wheelchair in a place where he could see everything.

"Easy, you have that little-girl look in your eyes."

Shelby checked the brake on the wheelchair, then looked at Brendan. "Join me?"

Brendan looked uncertainly at his father and she didn't know which was more precious to her, having him want to join her, or his being concerned about leaving his father alone.

Shelby took his hand in hers. "It'll be all right, Brendan. He can watch."

"Go on with you." Danny waved them on to the entrance of the ride.

Brendan wasn't that crazy about going on a roller coaster ride. Never having been given a chance to build up an immunity for them as a boy, the prospect of facing this kind of ride as an adult wasn't overly tempting. Only she was.

"Okay." He relented, looking up to the very top of the ride. "Just this once."

Shelby was already dragging him off to the end of the line. "Once is all I ask."

And once will never be enough, he thought.

When they finally got to the front of the line, Shelby lowered herself into a replica of a hollowed-out log. Stretching her feet out in front, she waited for Brendan to join her. He sat down behind her, his legs bracketing hers.

"You realize, of course, that this could lead to other things," he whispered against her ear, snaking his arms around her waist.

"Not in public." She laughed. "But if you could hold on to that thought another few hours, I'll be more than happy to oblige."

She made him laugh even as she made him want. The fluttery feeling in the pit of his stomach was as much caused by the woman as the ride.

The ride was fast, bumpy, full of sharp turns and exhilarating. He held her tightly against him as they suddenly flew down the long flume, plunging rapidly into the waiting waters.

Shelby shrieked as the sensation sailed through her. Brendan's legs tightened around hers as they plummeted. She turned, her hair slightly wet from the spray of water that flew around them when they landed.

"How are you holding up?" The words came out in a gasp of air.

He laughed and kissed her without thinking. "It's a little like making love with you."

"I take that as a compliment of the highest order." Within a moment they had traveled back to the starting point. Attendants dressed as lumberjacks stood ready to help everyone off and usher in a new crowd.

Brendan got out first and took her hand. "Want to do it again?"

She stumbled and then got her footing. "What, take the ride or make love?" One of the lumberjacks looked at them, then grinned and went back to helping people out.

"Both," Brendan said.

"I'll settle for the latter." She linked her arm through his. "The line's too long for the first choice, at least now. Maybe it'll thin out after three."

He nodded, as surprised at his suggestion as she was. "Come on, we'd better get back to my father."

"Gladly."

He saw the pleased smile on her face, but said nothing. He felt too good to listen to an I-told-you-so.

Shelby had led him through wonderland. She always seemed to. Brendan couldn't remember when he had had as much fun, outside of the nights they shared. By the time they were in the car, driving home, they had put in seven hours at the park. Danny was dozing peacefully in the back seat.

Brendan cast a sidelong glance at her face. "Pretty pleased with yourself, aren't you?"

"In what way?" she asked innocently.

He took a turn that would lead down to his street. "I'd say in every way."

"Maybe." She couldn't keep the grin back. "You both had a great time today."

"And you?" he asked needlessly. Mostly, he realized, he just liked to hear the sound of her voice.

"I always have fun at amusement parks. How about a baseball game tomorrow? Angels are playing the Blue Jays at Anaheim Stadium. Personally, I don't think the Blue Jays have a prayer."

Brendan grinned. It was becoming easier and easier to do. "They wouldn't if you were pitching."

She looked at him, confused. "I don't know how to pitch."

Brendan cocked a brow at her. "I think you do."

Shelby settled back in her seat, a warm feeling generating through her. "You give very unusual compliments, Brendan."

He turned the wheel left, then brought the car to a halt in his driveway. "They fit the subject."

She glanced over her shoulder toward Danny. "If you help me put your dad to bed, maybe we can go on one more log ride tonight."

"What?"

She pretended to look disappointed. "Surely you remember your clever simile. Or was that all just talk?"

He remembered. "I never just talk."

She kissed him quickly before getting out. "I was counting on that."

Brendan would have sworn that he would have felt awkward, helping her get his father ready for bed. In all the time since he had walked into the hospital room, the two men had only brushed hands. Yet with Shelby casually directing him in what she needed done, it became easy. More than that, it was a bonding experience. Brendan touched the frail, worn skin. It felt leathery, old, as if it had been through so much.

Maybe he had, Brendan thought. Maybe he had been going through his own private hell while Brendan had been experiencing his.

Maybe it was time to forget.

"Danny-boy," his father whispered as Brendan began to edge his way out. Shelby had discreetly left the two of them together without Brendan realizing it until it was too late.

Brendan paused. "I thought you were asleep." Oddly, the self-consciousness was gone.

"Almost." The old man propped himself up weakly on one elbow. The day had worn him out. "I want to thank you."

Gratitude always embarrassed him. "It was Shelby's idea."

"Grand girl, Shelly," Danny agreed. He looked at his son knowingly. "But idea or no, you didn't have to come."

Brendan shrugged casually. "There was nothing else pressing I had to do."

Danny shook his head. He saw through the excuses. "Doesn't matter. A man can spend a great deal of time doing nothing. I should know." He sighed heavily, struggling up farther in the bed. "I never meant to hurt you, Danny."

"But you did." It wasn't an accusation this time. It was merely a fact.

"Aye, I did, and I'll always be ashamed of that. But I thought your mother, being as beautiful as she was, would have found someone soon after, someone who could have taken care of her properly."

He searched his son's face, looking for understanding. Looking for forgiveness.

"She was married to you." Without thinking, Brendan moved back into the room, until he stood next to his father's bed.

"I had divorce papers sent."

"She never signed them," he told Danny. "She loved you to the end."

The statement left Danny in awe. Tears shimmered in his eyes for the love and the woman that had been lost to him. "And I her, Danny. And I her." He wiped his eyes with the back of his hand and then settled against his pillow. "Thank you for giving me a chance to know you, Danny. It's more than I deserve."

Brendan didn't know what to say. Emotion threatened to close off his throat. He touched his father's hand. It communicated things words could not.

"Go to sleep. She's got a baseball game planned for us tomorrow."

"Knows how to tire a man out, that one," Danny said, his eyes already closing.

"That she does, Dad, that she does."

As Brendan walked out of the room he found Shelby leaning against the wall in the hallway, waiting for him. A look at her eyes told him that she surmised what had happened.

"C'mon," he said, taking her hand, "you said something about a log ride."

Shelby laughed as she ran up the stairs with him.

Chapter Sixteen

"**Y**ou're hogging the popcorn."

Brendan looked at Shelby sitting next to him on the sofa. "I am not."

"Yes, you are." Shelby reached over and shook the bowl he held on his lap. There was very little popcorn left in it. Shelby did her best to look serious. "I would have never expected it of you."

She didn't expect, he thought, amused. There were a lot of things he would never have expected of himself. If anyone had asked him two months ago what he thought were the chances that he would be spending a Sunday afternoon in his family room, sitting next to his father, watching an old Alfred Hitchcock movie and "hogging popcorn," he would have glibly answered, "When hell freezes over."

Well, apparently there was a thin coat of ice over hell and a band of angels was skating across it. Angels led by Shelby.

"I guess I am, at that." He surrendered the bowl to Shelby.

"Lucky for you two I made a lot." Shelby marched off to the kitchen.

"Lucky," Brendan echoed, watching her go.

That was the word to describe it, all right, he decided. That was the word to describe everything. Lucky. While he wasn't a hundred percent at peace yet, this was the closest to peace he could remember being since he was seven. Shelby kept hemming him in at every turn, engineering things so that he was forced to face his own demons. Forced to face the fact that, though he swore to the contrary, he had never stopped loving his father, never stopped wanting to be loved himself. She had ripped away the scab he had been hiding behind, bandaged the wound and literally ordered it to heal.

It didn't dare do otherwise.

Outside the family-room window, sheets of rain were falling steadily, an unexpected cloudburst in the middle of a sunny season. It had washed out their plans for the ball game. Shelby had come up with an alternative plan. He was beginning to believe that she always would. It was just as she had told him. Nothing ever rained on her parade. She carried an umbrella.

Shelby emerged from the kitchen. The bowl refilled to the brim, she handed it to Danny and sat down beside Brendan. He reached for her, slipping his arm around her shoulders and tangling his fingers in her hair.

Sensuality mixed with contentment. He had never known it could be this way.

A small, dark voice whispered in the corners of his mind, asking how much longer it would last. He pushed it aside. It could last.

It *would* last.

The dark voice receded, but didn't fade.

Shelby shivered as the credits for *The Birds* rolled onto the large-screen television. "And *that* is why I don't own a parakeet."

Brendan looked at her, puzzled. "Don't tell me that movie spooked you."

She dusted her hands over a napkin, ridding herself of the salt that still clung to her fingertips. "All right, I won't."

He couldn't believe it. "A grown woman like you?" He laughed.

She raised her chin and sniffed. "I wasn't a grown woman when I first saw that and I have a very healthy, active imagination.

A lazy, sexy grin spread over the corners of his mouth. "Yes, I know."

She pretended to ignore that, although a radiance spread within her chest, causing her heart to beat just a little faster.

"So, what'll it be next?" She walked over to the table next to the video machine. An eclectic array of videos was spread out, ranging from comedies to adventures to Westerns with a couple of thrillers thrown in for good measure. "I have a whole collection here to choose from."

Brendan rose to look over her shoulder at the video-tapes. At the first sign of rain, Shelby had driven over to the video store to rent a good selection before other customers had a chance to take them.

Brendan picked up one and began reading the back cover. "Why on earth did you rent so many?"

The answer was perfectly obvious. "I had no idea what you'd be in the mood for."

Temptation was something he found himself resisting with less and less frequency and success. Brendan laced his arms around her waist despite the fact that his father was only a few feet away and looking on with apparent pleasure. He lightly touched the outline of her ear with his lips. "I think you do," he whispered.

Shelby looked over to where Brendan's father sat, but Danny pretended to be busy reading the names that scrolled across the wide television screen. She smiled. Very few people cared who the fourth cameraman was on the crew of a movie. Danny was a darling man. As was his son.

"Got anything with music?" Danny called over after what he deemed was a respectable amount of time.

"How about *Yankee Doodle Dandy?*" Shelby held up the tape.

Danny's eyes narrowed as he looked over at the tape. "They didn't mess it up by sticking color into it, did they?"

Shelby shook her head. "Heaven forbid. I made sure to get the original black-and-white version."

"Bring it here, Shelly girl," he directed, gesturing with both hands, pleasure brimming in his voice.

"Here." She handed Brendan the tape. "You do the honors. I'm going to make some more popcorn."

Brendan approached the VCR and searched for the Play button. He had purchased the machine over two years ago. In that time he hadn't had one single occasion in which to use it. Shelby had changed that. Shelby had changed a lot of things, he thought.

He found the Play button and pressed it and was rewarded with the FBI warning flashing at him. Then the movie title appeared.

"Remember this one?" Danny asked as Brendan sat down on the sofa.

Brendan thought for a moment. "No."

"Sure you do," Danny insisted. Suddenly it seemed important that Brendan recall the day. "They were having a Jimmy Cagney festival at the Triboro Theater. I took you. You were four, maybe five." Danny peered intently into his son's face. "Remember?"

Something stirred in the faraway corners of Brendan's mind. A darkened room, perhaps a theater. And music. His father holding his hand, laughing, singing softly under his breath along with a bright, smiling man dancing in front of them. No, not in front of them. On the screen. Brendan smiled. "Yes, I remember."

Danny sank back in his chair, content.

Shelby stood quietly in the doorway, unnoticed. She blinked back an insistent tear. It came anyway, mingling with the corners of her smile.

Brendan began looking forward to his life, to evenings when they sat and ate dinner together as a family. To nights when she was in his bed, in his arms. To weekends when she planned things for the three of them. Hope, the commodity that had been in such short supply for most of his life, began to push forward, through the mounds of dirt, breaking through to reach out to the warmth of the sun.

And to grow.

Maybe, just maybe, Brendan began to think, things just might work out.

He was involved in a new case. This one concerned embezzlement. There were far-reaching consequences and extenuating circumstances of great import. But there was nothing more important to Brendan now than living and enjoying his daily life.

"So, we're finally going to get to the ball game, eh?" Brendan asked Shelby.

It was a rhetorical question. The tickets were in his pocket. The game was starting in less than two hours and the sun was obligingly shining outside. It was a gloriously perfect day.

She loved seeing him like this. Lately it was as if a dark shadow had been lifted from him. He was lighter, happier. Healed. "You're really looking forward to this, aren't you?"

"Yes." Brendan took a soda can out of the refrigerator and poured himself a glass, then took a long drink. "I am."

There was a faraway look in his eyes. There was something different about this ball game, she thought. When they had been rained out the last time, Brendan had seemed disappointed. Shelby had never seen him look disappointed before. Disapproving, yes, but never disappointed. What was there about a ball game that affected him this way?

"Why?" Something, maybe instinct, made her put her arms around his neck as she asked, as if to offer comfort against the words to come, the memory that was to emerge.

Brendan placed his hands on her waist and looked at her. "Did I ever tell you about the day he left?"

She shook her head. "No," she whispered, afraid of what might come.

"It was my birthday. He was going to take me to a ball game. I waited all day." He laughed softly at the futility of it. "Even after the game was supposed to start, even after it was dark, I waited, sure that he would come home, some impossible explanation on his lips, followed by a promise that he would make it up to me." He pressed his lips together, banishing the memory. "That's all I wanted, really, to hear that he didn't mean it. That he was sorry."

She saw the tears that he refused to release. Her heart broke. "Oh, Brendan."

He shook his head, forcing a laugh. "I don't know what came over me." He released her, stepping away. "I didn't mean to say anything. We'd better hurry up or we'll be late."

"He's ready," she told him as they walked to his father's room. "He's been ready for over an hour." Maybe he remembered that game he never managed to attend, too, she thought, and somehow wanted to make it up to his son now.

Shelby knocked once on Danny's door before pushing it open. "We're ready, Mr. Connery."

She thought it strange that the man didn't call out to her. She received her answer when they entered. Danny was on his bed, his body racked with spasms as he shook and jerked uncontrollably.

"Shelby?" An unspoken plea for help mixed with a question resounded in Brendan's voice.

Shelby ran to Danny, holding him down. "He's having a seizure. He shouldn't. The phenytoin should be enough." Shelby feared the worst, but refused to give in to it. "Call an ambulance. We have to take him to the hospital."

Brendan had the receiver in his hand and was already punching out the numbers 911.

The ride to the hospital was a blur of whirling lights and wailing sirens for Brendan. Shelby went into the ambulance with his father while Brendan followed behind them in his sedan. A thousand different emotions crowded in on him at once. He scarcely noticed the traffic whizzing by in the opposite direction, or any of the cars he passed. He was too busy struggling not to panic or surrender his soul to an all-consuming darkness that dwelled just beyond, waiting to claim him.

It was going to be all right.

It had to be. They had a ball game to go to. Brendan felt for the tickets in his pocket as if to assure himself that they were there. As if that was all it took to anchor his father to life.

He dragged a breath into his lungs and slowly let it out. There was nothing to worry about. He had just gotten a second chance. It couldn't be snatched from him so cruelly.

He brought the car to a screeching halt next to the ambulance. When he rushed through the automatic doors of the hospital emergency room, he was only seconds behind Shelby and the paramedics.

"Take him straight in," Shelby ordered the two men in white livery. They hesitated. "I'm a nurse. I used to work here."

The two men exchanged looks and hurried Danny into the treatment area, bypassing the registration desk. The clerk behind the desk rose to stop her, but the look on Shelby's face halted the woman in her tracks.

Shelby hurried through the inner doors, looking around for someone she knew on the staff. She had started out her nursing career at Harris in emergency and periodically had worked the frantic hours that were required down here when they were shorthanded.

The emergency-room physician, a tall, willowy man with a beard, took her arm, catching her attention. "Shelby, what are you doing here? I thought you had left the hospital for good."

Shelby pulled him toward the stretcher that Danny was on. "I've got a patient for you." Shelby struggled to keep the emotion from her voice. She'd do no one any good if she fell apart. She remembered what Dr. Hemsley had told her about the nurse who had given bits and pieces of herself away. That wasn't going to happen to her.

But what was she going to do if Danny died?

Shelby kept her voice steady. "He has a brain tumor and has been having convulsions for about the last twenty minutes. He's Dr. Hemsley's patient."

"Call him," the physician ordered a nurse who was standing by. The woman moved quickly to put through the call while two orderlies moved a weakly thrashing Danny to another gurney behind a curtained area.

How could she sound so cold, so impersonal, as if she was reciting a laundry list, Brendan wondered angrily. Was everything she supposedly espoused just for show? He didn't understand. All he knew was the raw fear that had a viselike hold on him.

He tried to think straight. "Shelby, what... ?" There was no more, just that. What? What could he do? What could anyone do to help?

Shelby turned and looked at Brendan. She understood. The anguish in his eyes mirrored her own. "Praying wouldn't hurt."

But a cold resolve had come over his heart. He looked at the man he had once more accepted into his life. Brendan's voice was flat. "It probably won't help, either."

Dr. Hemsley had given hurried instructions over the phone and was on his way. Dr. Jacobs, the neurosurgeon, was called in, immediate X rays were ordered and Danny was taken away from them.

Shelby and Brendan waited in the outer annex of the emergency room. Brendan paced, bumping into corners of chairs and tables. It was a totally inadequate place for the anguish that was racking him. He wanted to explode, to rail, to make someone pay.

He wanted his father to live.

Emotions that had been buried for years were exploding within Brendan. He felt like a high-pressure vessel that had developed a hairline fissure and was about to blow apart. Brendan had almost forgotten these feelings. He had been methodical at his metamorphosis. This was exactly why he had struggled to become what he was. Caring always led to this. To pain. He'd been a fool to believe that it could be any other way.

Shelby was at a complete loss. This was at once too personal and too devastating. Holding back her own tears, she tried to take Brendan's hand. He felt strangely remote, even though his fingers clutched hers. She was losing them both, she thought. She fought back panic.

"They'll do all they can, Brendan."

"Yes, I know."

His voice was hollow, distant. He was reverting back to the Brendan she had met in the hospital corridor so long ago. She couldn't reach him. She didn't know how. She could only love him and hope that was enough.

Dr. Hemsley came out to talk to them thirty minutes later, his expression drawn. Shelby knew it couldn't be good.

The doctor put a hand on Brendan's shoulder. It was meant to be a fatherly gesture of comfort. Brendan suffered it stiffly, waiting. "We're going to have to operate, Mr. Connery."

Shelby stepped in, confused. Was there hope, then? "I thought you said the tumor was inoperable."

"It is." Shelby began to speak, but the doctor continued. "There's been some swelling and it looks as if the tumor is going to rupture at any time. We need to put in a drain, possibly prevent it from—"

"What are his chances?" Brendan cut in.

Dr. Hemsley took a breath. "There is always a chance that—"

"What are his chances?" Brendan repeated, his voice cold.

"Slim."

Brendan closed his eyes, gathering whatever courage he had left. He was vaguely aware of Shelby's hand in his. "Do it."

Damn. It wasn't fair. It just wasn't fair. But then, he thought, his cynicism returning, who had ever said that life was fair? He knew that. He had just forgotten it for a little while.

When he opened his eyes, the doctor was gone. He was looking into Shelby's eyes. They were moist. He took her into his arms and held her, a fragment of the only prayer he knew echoing through his head.

They waited in the room where he had first been, gathering his nerve to see his father for the first time in twenty-three years. How long ago was that? A week? A year? A lifetime?

Brendan couldn't remember.

Shelby talked, offering hope, filling the gloom they both felt, marking time. The waiting room was empty today. There was no one to share their mutual tension, their mutual fears. They watched the entrance together, hoping and dreading.

"It's going to be all right," Shelby said for the umpteenth time. She said the words as much for her as for him.

"Sure it is." He laughed shortly, wishing he had a cigarette, wishing he had something to do with his hands, his mind. "He's too ornery to die like this. It's just his way of getting out of the bet."

She didn't follow. "Bet?"

He nodded. "He bet me that the Yankees were going to win the game." He was talking quickly now, as if to keep away any thoughts. "He was always a diehard Yankee fan. He liked to welsh on bets and—"

Brendan's voice died away as he saw the doctor enter the room. He looked at Shelby, a mute fear reentering his eyes. It was too soon for the doctor to be here.

Shelby was on her feet, her hand on Brendan's arm. "Doctor?" There was no need for her to ask anything further.

"Mr. Connery," Dr. Hemsley said very quietly, "I'm very sorry."

"What?" Brendan's breath caught in his throat. "What are you sorry about?"

"We did everything we could."

No, he wasn't going to listen to this. If he didn't hear, it wasn't so.

"Then he's—?" Shelby couldn't bring herself to say the word.

The doctor turned to her, compassion on his face. "He never regained consciousness. The tumor ruptured before we could operate. We put in a drain, but it was futile." He licked his lips. "I—"

Brendan waved away the doctor's words, turning away from him. He didn't want to hear any empty words of condolence. Danny Connery meant nothing to the man behind him. "I'm sure you tried your best."

It was a cold voice, the voice she had heard him first use when he spoke of his father.

Dr. Hemsley nodded, retreating. "I'll give you a little time. I'll be here if you need me."

Shelby tried to put her hand on his arm, but Brendan shrugged it away. "Leave me alone, Shelby."

"No, I won't."

He spun around, anger flashing in his eyes. "Look, if it hadn't been for you," he shouted, "none of this would have happened."

"Me?" she cried, astonished.

He wanted to hit something, break something. "You were there, prodding, pushing, making me believe. Making me go through it again."

Shelby swallowed, trying to deny the hurt. "You don't know what you're saying."

"Yes, I do. I'm a lawyer. I'm supposed to always know what I'm saying." He hit his fist against the wall, but it didn't help. "He did it to me again, damn him. He made himself a part of my life and then he left again."

And in his heart he knew that it would be the same with Shelby, if he allowed it. Well, he wasn't going to. He had paid enough.

"Right before a baseball game." He shut his eyes, wishing he could shut it all away. His laugh was harsh, cruel. "At least he's consistent."

She knew he was trying to use his anger to protect himself from his feelings.

"Look at me." She took hold of his arms. "It's all right to cry. It's all right to feel. He was your father."

Brendan pulled away, hating her, hating himself. Most of all, hating his father. "He doesn't automatically deserve love for being that."

"Maybe yes, maybe no. But he has it. It's in your eyes, even if you don't want to admit it." How could she make him see?

"Eyes, again." His mouth twisted in a cruel smile. "Maybe you should try a new line of work, Nurse Tyree. You seem to suddenly find yourself without a patient. Here." He thrust the car keys into her hand.

She stared at them, dumbfounded. "Where are you going?"

But he was already walking away from her. "I don't know."

She wanted to run after him, to hold him and cry with him. But she knew that he had to work this through for himself. Perhaps she had done too much to him as it was.

Shelby sat down on the sofa and cried.

Chapter Seventeen

Brendan called a cab from the hospital lobby. The driver dropped him off at his door. He stood there as the cab pulled away, but he couldn't bring himself to go inside. His father wouldn't be there. It was just the same way it had been when he was a child, when his father had left. He hadn't wanted to go home then, either, because the emptiness that assaulted him was unbearable.

Just the way it was now.

Fighting back his anger, Brendan got into his sports car and drove away. He wanted to be alone, alone with the horrible sense of abandonment he felt. He wanted to lose himself.

For a while he roamed the city streets, aimlessly turning down one street and up another. Somehow, unconsciously, he found himself driving toward Anaheim Stadium. When he arrived, the game was just getting out. As he pulled in to the parking lot, cars were queueing up to leave. He shut off his engine and watched the cars pulling out, the occupants driving toward their families, toward their homes.

Brendan sat and stared into space for a long time. The music from the car radio droned on in the background, playing old rock-and-roll songs he had first heard as a child. No, he had never been a child, he thought. He had never had the time. It had been stolen from him, just as his father had been.

The music stopped for a minute and the fast-talking deejay was back on the air. Brendan put his hand on the knob to turn it off.

"And this final score just in. Looks like the Yankees pulled out of their slump in the ninth, beating the Angels eleven to six. There're going to be a lot of unhappy Angels fans out there tonight, folks."

"You won the bet, Dad," Brendan said quietly to the emptiness. "You should have stuck around to collect."

Brendan folded his arms over the steering wheel, lowered his head and cried.

Shelby was worried sick. It had been hours since she had last seen Brendan. She fought the urge to call the police, or at least Tyler.

He was all right, she told herself. Brendan was all right. He was just grieving.

She had returned to Brendan's house after making preliminary arrangements at the hospital. She had absolutely no idea what Brendan wanted done about funeral preparations. That was his decision to make. She had done the best she could.

Part of her had hoped that he'd be home when she arrived. She hurried out of the car and quickly opened the front door. The stillness that greeted her told Shelby that he wasn't there.

Nerves stretched taut, she waited for him to return. And as she waited, she packed.

Brendan found her asleep on the living-room sofa by the conversation pit. She jerked awake as soon as he entered the room.

She rubbed her eyes to clear the sleep away. When she focused on her watch, she saw that it was after three. "I was worried."

He sank down next to her. He wasn't certain where or how to begin. "You shouldn't have been."

"No, maybe not." There was an edginess in her voice transcending the compassion she felt. She was hurting, too. Didn't he realize that? They were supposed to comfort each other, not back into corners and come out fighting. "But I did, anyway. Occupational habit, I suppose."

At a loss, she folded her hands in her lap, telling herself that it was time to go. What was she waiting for? An engraved invitation? She should have already gone. But she couldn't have left until she knew he was safe. Well, he was safe.

He noticed the suitcase under the coffee table. "What's that?"

"My suitcase." A look of confusion spread across his face. "I'm leaving."

Panic seized him. Not her, too. No, not her, too. But his voice was even as he asked, "Why?"

He didn't care. The tone of his voice told her that. Why had she told herself otherwise? Dr. Hemsley was right. She should have kept a professional distance. Now she was paying the price.

"You once said that you had no need of a nurse, and now with your father...gone..." She licked her lips, unable to continue for a moment. "Irene will have something else lined up for me by the end of the week."

He wanted to reach out and hold her, to tell her that she couldn't leave. He could only sit where he was. "So soon?"

Shelby rose, her suitcase in hand. "There're a lot of sick people who need care." She started to leave the room. Her legs felt as if they were made of lead.

Tell me to stay, damn you.

She knew he wouldn't. She stopped for a moment, telling herself that she was a complete idiot. "Will you be all right?"

No, he was never going to be all right again. "No. Not if you leave."

"Brendan, I..." She wanted him to ask her to stay, more than anything else in the world she wanted him to ask her. She didn't want to volunteer anymore. But if he did ask her now, it would be for all the wrong reasons.

He crossed to her and put his hands on her shoulders. "Shelby, I can't say this more than once. Don't go."

She bit her lip. "There's nothing I want more than to stay."

He saw the hesitation and it almost made him back away. But he had come too far. "But?"

Why didn't she just take her happiness and run? Because it wouldn't have been real, she told herself, and someday he would resent her for it. "But I don't want you confusing your emotions."

Brendan smiled sadly. "For the first time in twenty-three years, I think they're finally not confused. You helped sort them out. If you leave, they'll be a mess again." He lifted her chin with the tip of his finger until she looked up into his eyes. "Isn't that against some kind of nurse's oath, leaving behind a mess?"

She wanted to laugh, to cry. "I—"

"I'm not going to let you say no." Brendan took the suitcase out of her hand and let it drop to the floor. When she moved to retrieve it he took hold of her hand, stopping her. "We can keep doing this all night and I'll win."

Relief began to flood through her. She hadn't wanted to leave. "Oh?"

"I'm stronger." He took her into his arms. "Except without you."

But she was still afraid. "I can't fill the gap your father left behind."

"I'm not asking you to. I'm asking you to fill another kind of a gap. This one's been there a long, long time. I didn't even realize it was there until I saw you, trying to wrestle that food cart to the ground."

"I was pushing it," she corrected, but the warmth was returning to her limbs.

"You were *trying* to push it," Brendan allowed, kissing the top of her head. "Just as you push everything else around."

"I—"

He placed a finger to her lips, not letting her go on. Whatever she had to say would have to wait. "You've talked for the last two months. It's my turn now and I have a lot to say."

"All right, go ahead." She braced herself, knowing that whatever he did say, whatever came of this, they were going to work things out. They *had* to.

Now that he had her attention, he found it difficult. He forced himself to speak. It was never easy when it came from his heart. He had never wanted to be this vulnerable. He found he had to be in order to keep what was most precious to him. He had to risk opening himself up completely to her.

"First of all, I'm sorry I walked out on you at the hospital. I just needed some time alone."

Now that she knew he was sorry, no apology was necessary. "I know that."

"Yes." He smiled. "You would. That's what's so special about you, Shelby. You know. You understand. I can be me and you're still there, laughing, talking. Always talking." Shelby moved to feign a punch and he caught her fist in his hand. "Maybe even loving me just a little bit." Though he tried to hide it, he said the words hopefully.

"Maybe?" Shelby stared at him as if he was a complete idiot. "You haven't been paying very close attention lately, have you?"

"Yes, yes, I have." He pulled her closer to him, absorbing the heat, the softness of her body. "You've taught me to open up my heart. And now you're going to have to pay for it. You're not going to run from your responsibility, are you?"

She pretended to think it over. "What kind of a responsibility?"

"I love you, Shelby, and I don't want to live without you."

As much as she wanted to cherish this moment, she was still afraid that she was getting him on the rebound. "Brendan." She searched his face, afraid of seeing something she didn't want to see. "Are you sure you're not just reacting to—"

"My father's death?" He forced the words out. "No." Brendan shook his head slowly. "That's what I did in the hospital. But I've come to terms with it, at least for now. He was what he was. He couldn't help that any more than he could help having a brain tumor. I know that now.'' He smiled, threading his hands through her hair. "And I do have him to thank for bringing you into my life."

Shelby relaxed. It was going to be all right. "Keep talking."

He kissed her temple. "Besides, weren't you the one who said I didn't do anything I didn't want to?"

"Guilty as charged, counselor."

"I'm glad that's settled because I want to marry you." He kissed the surprised expression from her face, kissed her until she was too breathless to respond verbally. "After paying those weekly charges, I figure it's a lot cheaper than hiring you as a nurse, and I am suddenly in the need of a lot of close, personal nursing. Maybe even a back rub or two. How about it?"

She took a deep breath. "When do you need your answer?"

Would she turn him down? No, not if he kept showing her that he loved her. He knew her by now, knew love when he felt it and when he saw it as he did in her eyes. "You don't have to hurry."

Shelby tried to look solemn, but couldn't quite carry it off. "Is now soon enough?"

He grinned, framing her face in his hands just before he kissed her. "Now would be just right."

"And so is your proposal."

"Then it's yes?"

"Beyond a shadow of a doubt, counselor." It was the last thing Shelby said for quite some time.

* * * * *

This is the season of giving, and Silhouette proudly offers you its sixth annual Christmas collection.

SILHOUETTE

Christmas Stories

1991

Experience the joys of a holiday romance and treasure these heart-warming stories by four award-winning Silhouette authors:

Phyllis Halldorson—"A Memorable Noel"
Peggy Webb—"I Heard the Rabbits Singing"
Naomi Horton—"Dreaming of Angels"
Heather Graham Pozzessere—"The Christmas Bride"

Discover this yuletide celebration—sit back and enjoy Silhouette's Christmas gift of love.

Silhouette Special Edition

COMING NEXT MONTH

#709 LURING A LADY—Nora Roberts
Barging into his landlord's office, angry carpenter Mikhail Stanislaski
got what he wanted. But, for the hot-blooded artist, luring
cool, reserved landlady Sydney Hayward to his SoHo lair was
another story....

#710 OVER EASY—Victoria Pade
Lee Horvat went undercover to trap Blythe Coopersmith by gaining
her trust. She gave it too freely, though, and both were
caught...struggling against love.

#711 PRODIGAL FATHER—Gina Ferris
It wasn't wealthy, stoic Cole Saxon's wish to reunite with his prodigal
father; it was A-1 wish-granter Kelsey Campbell's idea. And from the
start, Kelsey proved dangerously adept at directing Cole's desires....

#712 PRELUDE TO A WEDDING—Patricia McLinn
Paul Monroe was a top-notch appraiser. Sensing million-dollar
laughter behind Bette Wharton's workaholic ways, he betrayed his
spontaneous nature and planned...for a march down the aisle.

#713 JOSHUA AND THE COWGIRL—Sherryl Woods
Cowgirl Traci Garrett didn't want anything to do with big shots like
businessman Joshua Ames. But that was before this persistent
persuader decided to rope—and tie—this stubborn filly.

#714 EMBERS—Mary Kirk
Disaster summoned Anne Marquel home to face the ghosts of the
past. With tender Connor McLeod's help, could she overcome
tragedy and fan the embers of hope for tomorrow?

AVAILABLE THIS MONTH:

#703 SOMEONE TO TALK TO
Marie Ferrarella

#704 ABOVE THE CLOUDS
Bevlyn Marshall

#705 THE ICE PRINCESS
Lorraine Carroll

**#706 HOME COURT
ADVANTAGE**
Andrea Edwards

#707 REBEL TO THE RESCUE
Kayla Daniels

#708 BABY, IT'S YOU
Celeste Hamilton

Silhouette Special Edition

is pleased to announce

WEDDING DUET
by Patricia McLinn

Wedding fever! There are times when marriage must be catching. One couple decides to tie the knot, and suddenly everyone they know seems headed down the aisle. Patricia McLinn's WEDDING DUET lets you share the excitement of such a time.

December: PRELUDE TO A WEDDING (SE #712) Bette Wharton knew what she wanted—marriage, a home ... and Paul Monroe. But was there any chance that a fun-loving free spirit like Paul would share her dreams of meeting at the altar?

January: WEDDING PARTY (SE #718) Paul and Bette's wedding was a terrific chance to renew old friendships. But walking down the aisle had bridesmaid Tris Donlin and best man Michael Dickinson rethinking what friendship really meant....

SSEWD-1

"INDULGE A LITTLE" SWEEPSTAKES

HERE'S HOW THE SWEEPSTAKES WORKS

NO PURCHASE NECESSARY

To enter each drawing, complete the appropriate Official Entry Form or a 3" by 5" index card by hand-printing your name, address and phone number and the trip destination that the entry is being submitted for (i.e., Walt Disney World Vacation Drawing, etc.) and mailing it to: Indulge '91 Subscribers-Only Sweepstakes, P.O. Box 1397, Buffalo, New York 14269-1397.

No responsibility is assumed for lost, late or misdirected mail. Entries must be sent separately with first class postage affixed, and be received by: 9/30/91 for the Walt Disney World Vacation Drawing, 10/31/91 for the Alaskan Cruise Drawing and 11/30/91 for the Hawaiian Vacation Drawing. Sweepstakes is open to residents of the U.S. and Canada, 21 years of age or older as of 11/7/91.

For complete rules, send a self-addressed, stamped (WA residents need not affix return postage) envelope to: Indulge '91 Subscribers-Only Sweepstakes Rules, P.O. Box 4005, Blair, NE 68009.

© 1991 HARLEQUIN ENTERPRISES LTD.   DIR-RL

"INDULGE A LITTLE" SWEEPSTAKES

HERE'S HOW THE SWEEPSTAKES WORKS

NO PURCHASE NECESSARY

To enter each drawing, complete the appropriate Official Entry Form or a 3" by 5" index card by hand-printing your name, address and phone number and the trip destination that the entry is being submitted for (i.e., Walt Disney World Vacation Drawing, etc.) and mailing it to: Indulge '91 Subscribers-Only Sweepstakes, P.O. Box 1397, Buffalo, New York 14269-1397.

No responsibility is assumed for lost, late or misdirected mail. Entries must be sent separately with first class postage affixed, and be received by: 9/30/91 for the Walt Disney World Vacation Drawing, 10/31/91 for the Alaskan Cruise Drawing and 11/30/91 for the Hawaiian Vacation Drawing. Sweepstakes is open to residents of the U.S. and Canada, 21 years of age or older as of 11/7/91.

For complete rules, send a self-addressed, stamped (WA residents need not affix return postage) envelope to: Indulge '91 Subscribers-Only Sweepstakes Rules, P.O. Box 4005, Blair, NE 68009.

© 1991 HARLEQUIN ENTERPRISES LTD.   DIR-RL

INDULGE A LITTLE—WIN A LOT!

Summer of '91 Subscribers-Only Sweepstakes
OFFICIAL ENTRY FORM

This entry must be received by: Nov. 30, 1991
This month's winner will be notified by: Dec. 7, 1991
Trip must be taken between: Jan. 7, 1992—Jan. 7, 1993

YES, I want to win the 3-Island Hawaiian vacation for two. I understand the prize includes round-trip airfare, first-class hotels and pocket money as revealed on the "wallet" scratch-off card.

Name _____

Address _____ Apt. _____

City _____

State/Prov. _____ Zip/Postal Code _____

Daytime phone number _____
(Area Code)

Return entries with invoice in envelope provided. Each book in this shipment has two entry coupons—and the more coupons you enter, the better your chances of winning!

© 1991 HARLEQUIN ENTERPRISES LTD.　　　　　3R-CPS

INDULGE A LITTLE—WIN A LOT!

Summer of '91 Subscribers-Only Sweepstakes
OFFICIAL ENTRY FORM

This entry must be received by: Nov. 30, 1991
This month's winner will be notified by: Dec. 7, 1991
Trip must be taken between: Jan. 7, 1992—Jan. 7, 1993

YES, I want to win the 3-Island Hawaiian vacation for two. I understand the prize includes round-trip airfare, first-class hotels and pocket money as revealed on the "wallet" scratch-off card.

Name _____

Address _____ Apt. _____

City _____

State/Prov. _____ Zip/Postal Code _____

Daytime phone number _____
(Area Code)

Return entries with invoice in envelope provided. Each book in this shipment has two entry coupons—and the more coupons you enter, the better your chances of winning!

© 1991 HARLEQUIN ENTERPRISES LTD.　　　　　3R-CPS